A Healthier You...

The word *shiatzu* is derived from two Japanese characters: *shi* meaning finger, and *atzu,* meaning pressure. Together, these characters express the simple but potent essence of this type of therapy —finger pressure.

The roots of shiatzu go far back in time to the simple, primitive action of rubbing a painful area of the body to obtain relief. Like acupuncture and zone therapy, it is based on the recognition that certain key points of the body are related through the nervous system to other areas of the body, and that the application of pressure to these points can have a positive effect on the related areas.

Thus, we present to you *Shiatzu: Japanese Pressure Point Massage,* a method that works—and one that can be put to immediate use either for maintaining your present good health, or for alleviating some malfunction. Since you yourself will be your own shiatzu specialist, we suggest the use of shiatzu for those conditions that antedate the advice of a doctor. Keep reading . . . you're on the road to better health!

SHIATZU

Japanese
Pressure Point Massage

by Anika Bergson
and Vladimir Tuchak

PINNACLE BOOKS NEW YORK

SHIATZU: JAPANESE
PRESSURE POINT MASSAGE

*Copyright © 1976 by Anika Bergson
and Vladimir Tuchak*

An original Pinnacle Books edition, published for the first time anywhere.

First printing/October 1976
Eighth printing/October 1984

ISBN: 0-523-42526-0

Cover illustration by Bill Maughan

Printed in the United States of America

PINNACLE BOOKS, INC.
1430 Broadway
New York, New York 10018

14   13   12   11   10   9   8

Contents

List of Illustrations

Shiatzu:
Japanese
Pressure
Point
Massage

Introduction

In 1973, after years of practicing different methods of attaining and maintaining good health (see *Zone Therapy*, Pinnacle Books), we came upon the work of Tokujiro Namikoshi, in which we learned about his brilliant theories of Japanese finger-pressure therapy. Out of curiosity, as well as out of our previously successful experience with zone therapy, we began to experiment. We have continued to do this, after those initial experiments, with great success. In the past year, we have extended our experimentations, with equal success, to our friends and others. It is as much out of their enthusiastic urgings as out of our concern for the dissemination of information on preventive self-help therapies that we decided to once again sit down to the task of writing and sharing this knowledge with others. As with our book on zone therapy, we have attempted in this work to bring together the available information in a simple format that can be used by the layman to select the most applicable material for his own therapy.

The word *shiatzu* comes from two Japanese characters, one meaning finger (*shi*), the other meaning pressure (*atzu*). Together, these characters express the simple but potent essence of this type of therapy—finger pressure. Shiatzu therapy, as it is practiced today, was evolved by Tokujiro Namikoshi, who has spent over forty years developing its theory and practice. During this time, he has helped over a hundred thousand people. By founding the Nippon Shiatzu School, he has assured the development and continuance of shiatzu for an ever-increasing, grateful public.

The roots of shiatzu go far back in time to the simple primitive action of rubbing a painful area of the body to obtain relief. Other roots, no doubt, connect shiatzu to both acupuncture and zone therapy. In all of these, there is the realization that certain key points in the body relate to other areas and that, by pressing these key points, areas of pain or disease can be positively affected. Furthermore, all of these theories recognize the innate healing and balancing mechanism of the human organism, and attempt to use the built-in bio-systems that nature has provided. Acupuncture uses needles, zone therapy concentrates principally on applying pressure to the hands and feet, and shiatzu employs its own type of pressure. It does not matter much that the key points might be called by different names—reflexes, acupuncture points, or shiatzu points. The seed of thought, basic to them all, is the same. The history of shiatzu then goes back to this deeper understanding of its essential nature. Thus we owe our thanks not only to Namikoshi but to the ancient Chinese and to the American pioneers of zone therapy as well.

The difference among the various treatments seems to lie in the kind of pressure treatment recommended by each method; yet, in all methods, results are obtained. To this day, no one quite knows why. We will not presume to impose on our readers' gullibility and suggest any kind of explanation whatever. Let it suffice for the reader, as it has for us, that the method under discussion works. Why it works is a matter for future scientists to unravel.

But if these methods have a common basis, why then, the reader may wonder, have we limited ourselves only to the shiatzu way? We have done so because of the simplicity of the method and because a book that attempted to deal with all of these methods at once would be confusing and difficult to use. Our purpose here is to elucidate a method that *works*—one that can be relatively simply put to immediate use for either maintaining one's present good health or for alleviating some malfunction.

Of course, the medical profession is to be sought for any serious condition, as well as for consultation on any question regarding your health that you might have. Shiatzu can help serious disorders in some cases, but this is only true when a professional shiatzu expert is in charge of the situation. Even then, most shiatzu practitioners work closely with the medical profession. Since you yourself will be your own shiatzu specialist, we suggest the use of shiatzu for those conditions that antedate the advice of a doctor.

1

An Ounce of Prevention

Humanity has always suffered from disease and daily ills, but there seems to be a greater incidence in this twentieth century—particularly in the highly industrialized countries—of certain types of diseases, such as cancer and heart disease, as well as conditions of hypertension and anxiety. This is in addition to a whole array of minor aches and pains. Great strides have been made in the medical profession. We live longer. We lose very few newborns in the process of modern childbirth. We have controlled many of the contagious diseases that used to ravage whole populations. We have highly advanced technology to aid doctors both in diagnosis and in the relief of symptoms. Our surgical methods have advanced to the point where we can transplant a heart or kidney from one human being to another. There are advances that the average layman has never even heard of—advances that, to some of us, would belong to the realm of fantasy or magic. Yet we are ill.

For a people that is supposedly as healthy as we are here in the United States, we consume more prescription and nonprescription medicines than all the technologically underdeveloped countries put together. We take pain relievers, laxatives, antihistamines, sleeping pills, diet pills, tranquilizers, stimulants, decongestants, antibiotics, and a whole gamut of other medicines. We are constantly either waking ourselves up or putting ourselves to sleep. Indeed, when one uses the term "drug culture," we personally find it difficult to separate that term from the whole of American culture. In some distant-future history book, we could be aptly named the Pill-Popper Culture!

The reasons are many. In spite of assurances from our government bureaus that we are the best-fed population in the world, we ail. It is true that we have available in this country the best and most plentiful of good foods, but we convert those good foods into junk and devour it. Instead of whole grains, we consume highly processed ones from which a good deal of the nutritive value is taken. Instead of fresh fruits and vegetables, we eat precooked, processed ones and overcook them to boot, so that the few vitamins and minerals that were left in the packages are almost totally gone by the time we get them into our bodies. We prefer convenience foods, those prepackaged mummies with all their preservatives and chemical additives. We have our colas, coffee, and our sugar-rich, fruit-type drinks, which our children pour into themselves with the assurance on the labels that they are getting all their daily vitamins. Beyond this, we have broken the natural food cycle with all our pollutants that have entered the air we breathe, the water we drink, and the soil in which we grow our foods.

And this is not all. In our cities, we have surrounded ourselves with intrusive noises that bombard us constantly—and we wonder then why we are nervous! We drive everywhere, using our legs and backs only to prop us up on the soft cushions of our automobiles. We work, most of us, at jobs we detest, jobs that we feel anyone else could do, so that our self-value is considerably diminished. Yet, we believe, we have the best of all possible worlds. And, indeed, in many ways, we do. But, certainly, it is possible to improve that world by improving one's eating habits, by exercising, and by using the simple techniques of shiatzu to put the body back into its natural balance.

We have ignored our bodies too long. They are amazingly adaptable organisms and capable, obviously, of taking a great deal of punishment. But our bodies and minds have limits. When we ignore these limits, we become ill. Perhaps the most important part of your shiatzu work will make you aware once again of the needs of your own body. This seems so obvious, yet so many people think of their bodies in the same way they think of their cars—they are vehicles that simply carry "us" around, as if "we" were separate from our bodies! With shiatzu, by touching your own body, you can begin to come back to an awareness that your body is you, that it deserves the same kind of care and consideration that you might demand for your emotional needs. Your whole mental condition will be greatly improved by your newly acquired body awareness.

Touching is of great importance and is a language in itself. It is a language that the body, at a primal level, understands and responds to. Let us give only one example of this. We do not plan to burden the reader with any further case histories, since we feel they only impose on our reader's credibility and in no real way provide him with proof of the method under discussion. Such proof can only come from the reader's own experiments with the method.

Our own experience with the importance of touching came from our regular visits, years ago, to a chiropractor who was giving us spinal manipulations. We greatly looked forward to these visits, which seemed to loosen up all the accumulated tensions in the neck and back that occurred during the week. At some point, however, during these treatments, the chiropractor began to use a small metal device in place of his hands. This practice continued for a period of about two months. We began to feel dissatisfied and impatient with the treatments, feeling that he was just not doing what he had been doing all along.

He assured us that the device could provide deeper and more long-lasting effects than he could possibly achieve with his hands and, no doubt, he was quite right, but we were not convinced. It took us about two months to realize that what we missed was the *touching* by another human being. It was important and necessary to our treatment, not just on a psychological level but also on the physical level. Our bodies wanted to be touched. Once the chiropractor returned to his regular routine, using his hands, our dissatisfaction disappeared and we began to progress again.

So, by touching your body, by caring for it, your health will already improve simply from the attention you are giving yourself. This is perhaps one very basic reason why the methods of shiatzu and other pressure treatments work.

At a more scientific level, shiatzu works because by applying pressure to key areas, the congestion of lactic acid that accumulates in the muscle tissue is released. The process is complex, but relatively simple to understand. After digestion, the nutrients we receive from the foods we eat are converted into glycogen and distributed by the blood to the muscles. The glycogen then combines with oxygen from our lungs and com-

8

bustion takes place, which produces energy for our muscles. But, as with any process of combustion, there is a residue—in this case, lactic acid—that causes fatigue.

An overaccumulation of this residue can be taken care of by the simple act of resting, during which time the lactic acid is removed by the bloodstream through the veins, and fresh glycogen is brought in by the arteries. However, with lack of sufficient rest, or with long-term stress, in which case even rest is a time of tension, the lactic acid accumulates. If uncorrected for a long enough time, the muscles begin to contract improperly, bringing on disturbances in all other parts of the body. Thus, we become sick.

With shiatzu treatments, pressure is put on these fatigued muscles and as much as eighty percent of the lactic acid can be reconverted into glycogen, so that the cause of the illness is eliminated.

In effect, what shiatzu does is to work with the natural curative powers of the body itself. Partly why the human body can take the immense amount of neglect and punishment that it does is because of the many systems inherent to it that work toward achieving a balance. Shiatzu works and in hand with those systems to generate a speedier cure and not simply to alleviate symptoms. Naturally, one treatment of shiatzu will not achieve the desired results, especially for people who have long neglected their bodies and its imbalances; but, given time, the balance will be achieved and relief obtained.

One might wonder what the difference is between shiatzu and simple massage. While massage has great benefits, its effect is often superficial, whereas the effects of shiatzu are deep and long-lasting. In massage, even deep massage, the muscles are manipulated in such a way that, while relief from soreness and stiffness is obtained, the results are usually temporary. This is because the cause of the condition has not been reached—the cause being a long-accumulated fatigued condition with the resultant buildup of wastes in the muscle tissue. Shiatzu reaches down to the cause by touching the points at which this accumulation occurs. Thus it is dispelled and long-lasting results are obtained.

But the essence of shiatzu is the *prevention* of illness. Its primary purpose is to stimulate the body's own innate powers of healing and balancing. Its use can only bring pleasurable sensations, and the results are often remarkable. There are no harmful or unpleasant side effects as there sometimes are with medicines. It is a system of therapy that helps the body to help itself, and is in complete harmony with nature. None would claim that shiatzu is a medicine. It works out of basic human instincts to *prevent* the onset of illness. Using shiatzu on a daily basis, a few minutes a day, will keep the body in such a condition that symptoms of illness that might require a doctor's attention will simply not develop.

Shiatzu is suitable to anyone, from young children to the very aged; and, best of all, it can be used anywhere, anytime, since no tools, other than your own hands, are ever involved. You can perform most of the procedures on yourself, although it is more convenient at times to work with a partner to reach points on the back. We have found it convenient in our daily shiatzu treatments to work first alone and then alternately with each other. With five to ten minutes of treatments a day, best done in the morning—with the exception of one treatment we perform at bedtime to relax us—you can maximize your energy and good health to a point you never believed possible. But don't just take our word for it. Try it!

2

It's All in the Hands

Look at your hands. Notice them carefully. These are the tools you will be using to restore your body to its natural balance and health. What could be simpler than your own hands? Or what more complex? Notice particularly your thumbs and fingers. Are your thumbs straight and hard? Or are they gentle and naturally curved? If they are of the former, you will have to learn to use them gently because they will be capable of exerting great pressure. If they are gently curved thumbs, you will have to learn to strengthen them so that more pressure can be gotten from them. Your thumb is your most valuable tool, but you will also use three fingers—your index, middle and ring fingers—for some treatments. On occasion, you will use the palm of your hand. However, the thumb will be employed most frequently in your exercise of shiatzu.

Your shiatzu treatments will affect the functioning of every system in your body from the glands to the muscles and organs, even the skeleton. Whether you use shiatzu to correct an already-present malfunction or as a daily health measure to maintain your present good health, its effect can only be beneficial and pleasant. You have only to learn how to use your hands on the key points as illustrated in this book to help you achieve whatever goal you have set for yourself.

We strongly urge you to start your shiatzu treatments by first carefully studying figures 1 and 2 for the location of the main shiatzu points. Follow this by giving yourself a full treatment as outlined in chapter 3. By doing this, you will be able to quickly assess what areas are most in need of your attention. A little more time will be involved in these first few treatments you give yourself, but it will be well worth it. We recommend your doing the full treatment for perhaps two weeks. Then you may cut down the time of the treatments, if you so wish, by doing the five-minute daily treatment recommended at the end of chapter 3, along with any others that you have chosen for specific conditions.

Here are some basic rules for you to follow:

1. Always choose a time of day when you feel unhurried and comfortable. Although it is best to start your day off right with a shiatzu treatment in the morning, we recognize the variety of ways in which people meet the day. Some of us simply find it too difficult to give up the extra ten minutes of sleep that an early-morning treatment would take. Others awaken with their minds already racing forward to the activities of the day ahead and would find a treatment an interference rather than a benefit. So we feel you yourself must be your own judge as to when the treatment will most help you. The important thing is that you be able to concentrate your attention fully on what you are do-

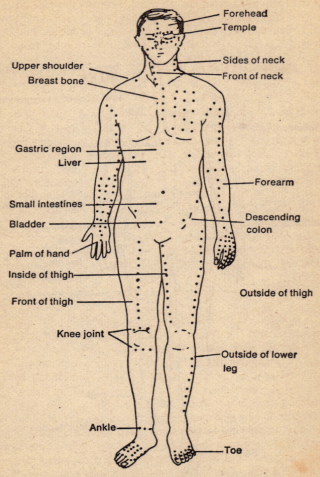

Fig. 1: Location of Shiatzu Points: Front

13

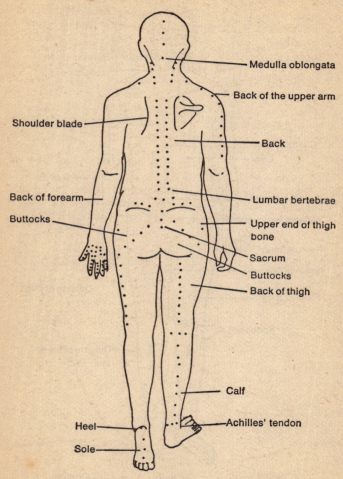

Medulla oblongata

Back of the upper arm

Shoulder blade

Back

Back of forearm

Lumbar bertebrae

Buttocks

Upper end of thigh bone

Sacrum

Buttocks

Back of thigh

Calf

Achilles' tendon

Heel

Sole

Fig. 2: Location of Shiatzu Points: Back

14

ing. Leave the other distractions aside. You should feel unhurried and fully comfortable both mentally and physically. While it is best to wear as little clothing as possible, choose what is comfortable for you and, by no means, allow yourself to get chilled.

2. Be aware of your posture. At no point take an awkward or uncomfortable position. When sitting, sit erect with your spine straight but not rigid. When reclining, use a pillow to support your head and neck.

3. Breathe deeply a few times before you start your treatment. This will help calm you and turn your attention inward to your body.

4. Be sure your fingernails are trimmed so that the nails do not gouge the skin.

5. Always push with the ball of your thumbs and fingers. (See fig. 3) Do not push with the tip. Apply pressure evenly and gently, except where strong

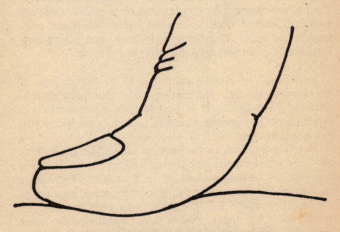

Fig. 3: Correctly applying pressure

pressure is recommended. Regulate your pressure with your own breathing, always being aware of your own responses. If even slight pressure on a point brings pain, release. You have plenty of time to make up for the time you have neglected your body. You do not need to punish yourself. Time and attention to yourself through your shiatzu treatments will work out the sore points; so be patient.

6. Relax while keeping your mind concentrated on what you are doing. If you feel your attention wandering or if you are unable to keep yourself in a relaxed state, stop. Never force yourself to continue treatment at a given time. Shiatzu will only help you if you can flow peacefully with it. Tomorrow is another day. If you stop your treatment when nervous or distracted, you will feel better about giving yourself a treatment the next day than if you force yourself to continue.

7. Never continue treatments longer than advised. Five to seven seconds of pressure on a point is always sufficient except when otherwise indicated. Your neck area is the most sensitive and, in that area, we recommend only three seconds' duration of pressure.

You must be your own judge as to the degree of pressure you exert. Remember only that pain should indicate your limits. It is best if your pressure brings you to a point between pleasure and pain, as when you rub a sore muscle.

For those points to be pressed along the back, it is best and most convenient if you have someone to do it for you. However, we recognize that not everyone is so fortunate. Consequently, a compromise has to be made. If you are fairly supple, you may be able to reach most of these points by reaching over your shoulder and using your middle and index fingers in place of your thumb. The lower middle back can be reached, using the thumb, by reaching back and around. If you lack the flexibility to do the back treatments and cannot get someone to help you, you will have to forego this part of the treatment. Do not strain yourself to reach points on the back, however. Remember, you must always be comfortable. It is better to neglect an area than to go into contortions that could undo all of your labors.

One of our friends, who lives alone, devised for himself what he, at least, feels to be an ingenious device with which he is able to reach all the points on his back. While we have strong reservations about his method, we pass it along to you with his assurances that he has used it without harm for over a year. Using a pegboard, he attached rounded rubber erasers to it at exactly those points on his back he could not reach. He then backs up against these thumblike protrusions to apply the gentle pressure his back requires. He calls it instant shiatzu. We call it shiatzu out of desperation!

3

The Full Treatment

Giving yourself the full shiatzu treatment will take some time until you have become familiar with the points as illustrated in figures 1 and 2. Study the diagrams well, along with the individual charts in this chapter that illustrate the points in the areas you will be working on. We strongly urge you to use the full treatment, particularly in the first two weeks of your experimentation, and as often as possible after this initial period. Once you have learned the points to touch and have found the most comfortable way to reach them all, the time involved will not be longer than about thirty minutes.

We find it most convenient to begin at the bottom and work up. Look at the charts for the feet in figures 4, 5, 6, and 7. These are the points you must touch. Now look at your own feet and locate the points. Sit comfortably in a chair or at the edge of a bed, putting one foot upon your knee. First, press each toe on all points three times. Your thumb should be on the top of

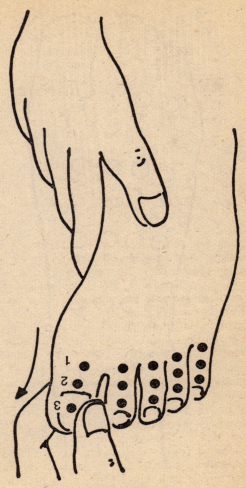

Fig. 4: Points on toes

19

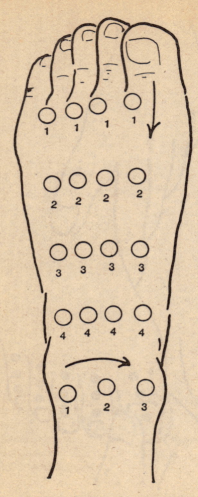

Fig. 5: Points on instep

20

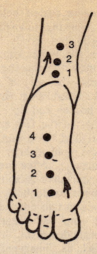

Fig. 6: The sole of the foot and the Achilles' tendon

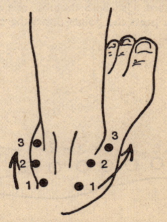

Fig. 7: Points on ankle

the toe with your fingers curled below. Begin at the base of the big toe, working toward the little toe of each foot. Press gently but firmly. Next, with your thumb, press between the bones on your instep three times on each point, moving from the base of your toes toward the ankle. Press the sole of your foot on the four illustrated points. Establish a rhythm. Next, press on both sides of the ankles and up along the Achilles' tendon. These exercises of the feet are especially helpful when you are fatigued. You can use them during the day when you feel your energy level falling. Just slip off your shoes during a coffee break and see if you don't feel as though you have recovered your strength and stamina! Remember to do both feet. At the most this treatment takes one or two minutes.

The next step in your full treatment is to apply pressure to all the points down the side of the calf from your knee to your ankle as illustrated in figure 8. Work down the leg from just below the kneecap to the points above your foot. Use both thumbs, one on top of the other, as you press the points down the calf, alongside the shinbone.

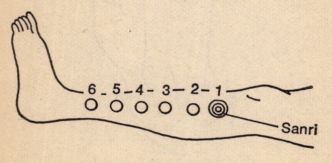

Fig. 8: Front of calf
22

Using both thumbs again, press the points on the back of the knee and down the middle of the calf (fig. 9). Remember to do both legs and to keep your muscles relaxed.

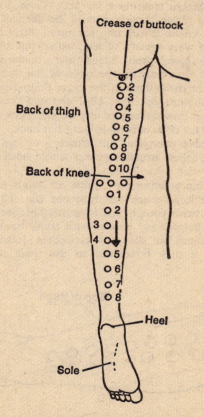

Fig. 9: Points on back of leg

Again, beginning at the top of the thigh, press all points illustrated in figures 10, 11, and 12. Start with a light pressure upon the groin point, using the flat palm of your hand. This can best be done in a sitting position unless you are fortunate to have someone administering your shiatzu treatment for you. Then you can just lie back. Your fingers should be turned down toward your knees. Push on this point three times, gradually and very gently. Then, with both thumbs, side by side now, their edges just touching, put pressure on those points on the front of the thigh (fig. 10). Press then the points on the inner thigh (fig. 11), the outside of the thigh (fig. 12), and end this treatment by going down those points on the back of the thigh (fig. 9). This accomplished, lie back, stretch your arms above your head and shake your legs vigorously several times, stretching your whole body at the same time.

In a standing position now, press all points as illustrated on the lower back and buttocks (fig. 13). Use your thumbs, with your hands forward. This treatment is especially helpful for people with weak backs who suffer from slight but constant backaches. It will help such people if they remember to use their stomach

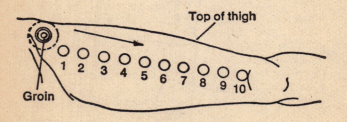

Fig. 10: Top of thigh

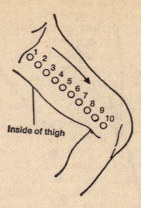

Fig. 11: Inside of thigh

muscles to do a lot of the work in keeping the body erect. Too often, we rely on the back muscles to do the whole job. A sagging, protruding stomach puts an extra burden on these muscles. Develop these stomach muscles. You will not only feel better, but look better too.

Now, either lying or sitting, press all points on the abdomen as shown in figure 14, using the index, middle, and ring fingers of both hands. Press each point for the duration of three seconds only and repeat the application three times on each point. That accomplished, place the palm of one hand over the pit of your stomach, located just above your waistline, and press lightly on this area for thirty seconds. Moving slightly down and to the left, again with the palm of your hand, press gently on the four points in figure 15 over the descending colon.

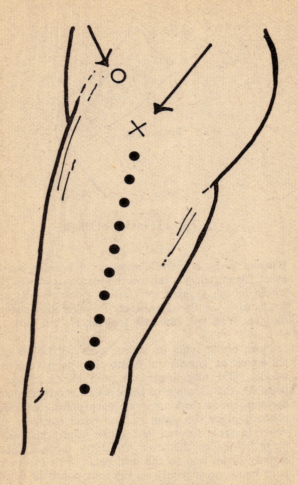

Fig. 12: Outside of thigh

26

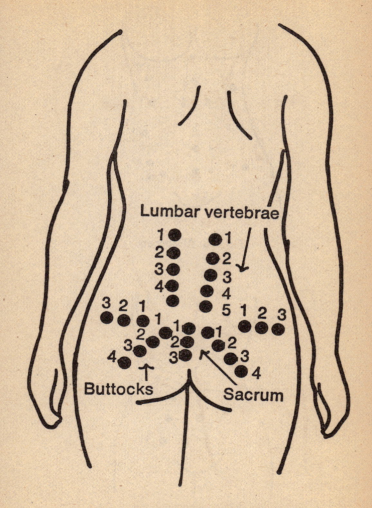

Fig. 13: Back, buttocks & sacrum
27

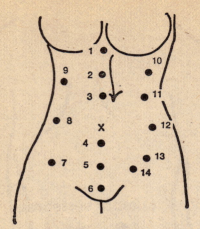

Fig. 14: Abdomen

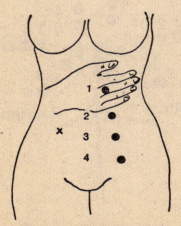

Fig. 15: Descending colon

28

The next series of treatments will be best accomplished in a sitting position. Reaching over your shoulder with the opposite hand, use your three fingers to press on the points illustrated in figure 16. Do not strain. Depending on your flexibility, you may or may not be able to reach all the points. Remember that it is better to forego a treatment that might make you uncomfortable. The last thing we want is for you to pull a muscle trying to do something that is supposed to help you. If you have a partner, this is a treatment in which his or her assistance is advised.

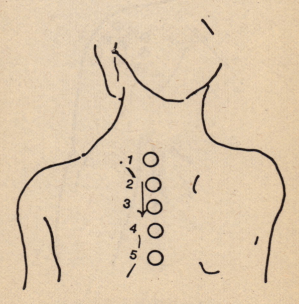

Fig. 16: Shoulder blades

29

Next, move to your shoulder area and, with your thumb, press the nine points in figure 17. Press all points on the arms and hands for three to five seconds three times each. Move down the points on the outer side of the upper arm, then down the inner side (figs. 18 and 19).

Fig. 17: Shoulder

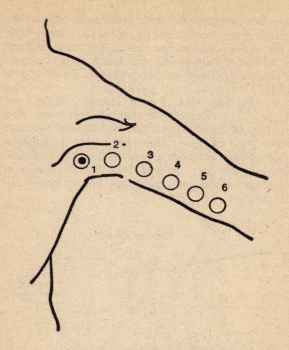

Fig. 18: Inside of upper arm

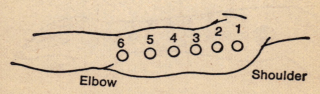

Fig. 19: Outside of upper arm

31

Elbow bent, gently rest your forearm in your other hand. With your thumb, gently press the nine points down the inside of your forearm to the wrist. Repeat on the middle-section points and finish with the same procedure on the third row of points as illustrated in figure 20. Turn your hand palm-down and press the points on the back side of your forearm, using your thumb (fig. 21). Remember that wherever you find pain in any of these treatments, lighten the pressure and make note of these points for future treatments. Any sign of pain indicates a problem area and, should you decide to use only the brief daily shiatzu treatment, include these painful areas until they are no longer noticeably painful.

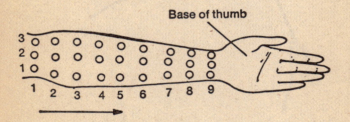

Fig. 20: Inside of forearm

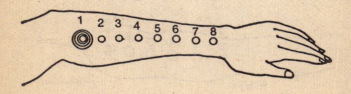

Fig. 21: Outside of forearm

The next area for your attention is your hands. Study figure 22 and, starting at the wrist, work downward on the points on the back of the hand. Use your thumb, balancing your palm on your thigh so you can exert some pressure. Then, using your thumb on one side and your index finger on the other, press the points on the outer edges of your fingers simultaneously. Do one finger at a time, first pressing the outer edges with two fingers, then the central points with the thumb alone. It is especially important that the outer-edge points be pressed at the same time. When you have finished pressing these points, turn your hand palm-up and press firmly the three points illustrated in figure 23. Press the middle point three times with strong pressure.

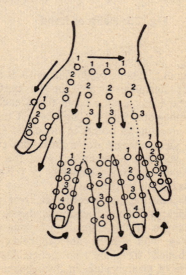

Fig. 22: Hand & fingers

33

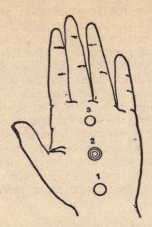

Fig. 23: Palm of hand

Rest a moment. Then, beginning with the topmost point on your sternum, located in the center of the chest, press these five points three times each, moving downward with your thumb (fig. 24). Continue the treatment by pressing all points in the chest area. Work out from the sternum and down from the collarbone. Be sure that you are pressing between the ribs. You must not press on the ribs themselves or push so vigorously that you inhibit your breathing.

Periodically, during the treatments, rest a moment and breathe deeply. In the beginning, this is especially important because of the intensity of your concentration. Gradually, you will be able to relax more and gain greater benefit from the treatments. Also, remember to be aware of your breathing during treatment and try to work together with it, establishing a rhythm.

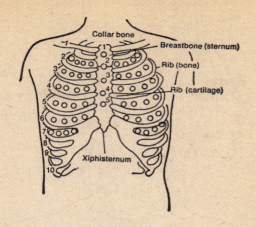

Fig. 24: Chest

Now you are ready to move up to the most sensitive part of your shiatzu treatment—the neck. Press only three seconds in any part of the neck and be gentle with your pressure.

With your fingers behind the neck, use your thumb to press in a descending fashion the points first on the front of the neck, then the side, and finally the back. In pressing the points on the back of the neck, use three fingers (fig. 25). Again, we remind you to do both sides, as with all other treatments. Now with your fingers on top of your head, place your thumb over the medulla oblongata (fig. 26), located at the base of your skull in the depression you find there. Press, gradually increasing your pressure and using a slight kneading movement, three times for five seconds each time. Now press the three points on the back of the head above the medulla oblongata.

35

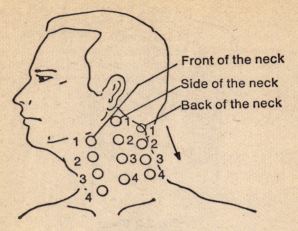

Front of the neck

Side of the neck

Back of the neck

Fig. 25: Neck

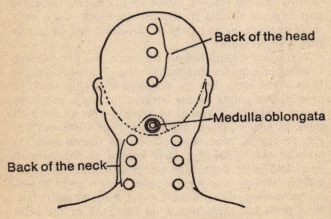

Back of the head

Medulla oblongata

Back of the neck

Fig. 26: Back of head & neck

36

With one hand, using either your thumb in a sideways approach or your three fingers, whichever is easier for you, press the six points on the top of your scalp (fig. 27). Move from your hairline back and repeat this procedure three times. Then, with the three fingers of both hands, press the points moving out from this central row, starting at the back of the head this time, and moving forward (fig. 28). Do this procedure only one time.

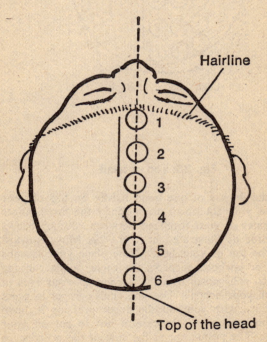

Fig. 27: Top of head

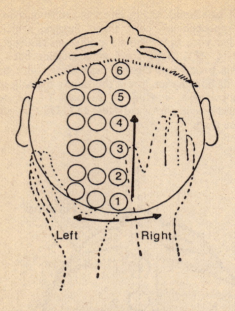

Fig. 28: Top of head

Rest the fingers of one hand lightly on top of your head. Use your thumb to press gently the three points in the center of your forehead between your eyebrows and hairline as illustrated in figure 29. Move upward toward the top of your head. Now place your thumbs under your jawbone to press the three points running parallel to your nose from the corners of your eyes to the top of your nostrils. Use your index finger to press these points, with your middle finger pressing it down for a firmer pressure. Be careful not to cut off your breathing. The points are at the side of the nostrils, so you should be able to continue breathing normally.

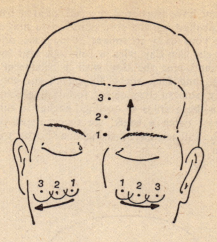

Fig. 29: Forehead & cheeks

With your three fingers, press along the bottom of your cheekbones (fig. 29). For the points just below and above the eye (fig. 30), again use your index finger with your middle finger pressing down on it. Press each of these points only once and be careful not to press on the eyelid itself. Move to the side of the eye then and press the three points along the temple (fig. 31). Use your thumbs for this, with your fingers resting on your scalp. Now, rub your hands together to warm your palms. Lie back and relax. Take a few deep breaths. Place your warmed palms over your eyes, taking care not to touch the eyeballs themselves. Your palms should form a cup over the eyes. You may stay in this position for as long as you like with your eyes closed. If done at bedtime, you will surely fall into a deep and restful sleep.

After you have mastered the full shiatzu treatment and have worked out the sore points, you may wish to abbreviate your daily treatment as we have done. We usually begin our day with a full foot and lower-leg treatment and end the day with a treatment of the head, neck, and face areas. If you choose to do this short daily shiatzu treatment, follow the same procedures for these areas as outlined earlier in this chapter. At least twice a week, we recommend you give yourself the full treatment, using this shorter treatment in between.

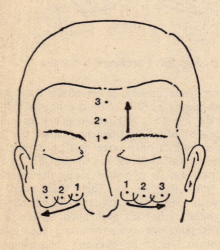

Fig. 30: Eyes

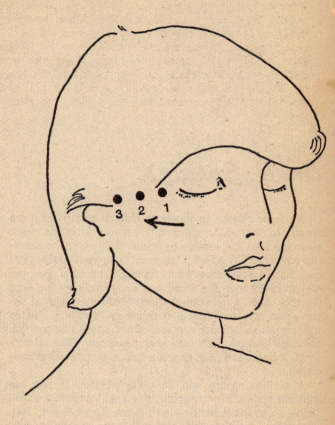

Fig. 31: Temples

4

Ankle Sprains

We have chosen to illustrate shiatzu treatment for a sprain in the ankle since this seems to be the most common area for sprains to occur. But, using the previous chapter ("The Full Treatment") as your guide, you can treat a sprain anywhere it might occur if you use the procedures in the same way as we will outline here for the ankle. Contusions—deep bruises or injured tissue—can also be treated in this way. Swelling and/or inflammation indicate contusions and should be treated, harmless though they may seem, because their aftereffects, if neglected, can develop into a more serious condition.

A serious sprain will be quite painful. If you are treating a sprain for yourself, our usual warnings about pain—to touch it lightly—will prove unnecessary. But, if you are administering shiatzu therapy to another person, remember to watch his reactions. Your touch should be the lightest possible.

Take the injured ankle in one hand and press lightly

with your palm. Hold your palm on the affected area until it feels less feverish and the throbbing subsides. You are now ready to press the shiatzu points, first on the ankle itself, then on the areas surrounding the ankle. Press the three points on either side of the ankle (fig. 32), each point three times for no more than three seconds. Follow this by pressing the three points on the Achilles' tendon (fig. 33). For this treatment, press first on the topmost point and work down, always working *toward* the sprain, not away from it. Next, starting at the topmost point, press the eight points on the back of the calf, again three times each for three seconds each (fig. 34). Now press the points along the shinbone, on the outer side of the calf of the affected leg (fig. 35). Finish by giving the complete foot treatment, beginning with pressing the points on the toes, then the instep, sole of the foot, and top of the foot, remembering to always work toward the sprain. (See figs. 4, 5, and 6.) Relief should be obtained. You or the patient should rest the ankle for at least thirty minutes after the treatment.

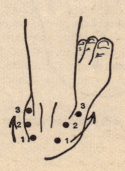

Fig. 32: Points on ankle

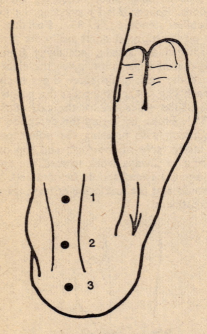

Fig. 33: Achilles' tendon

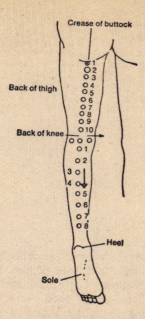

Fig. 34: Points on back of leg

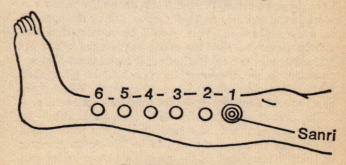

Fig. 35: Front of calf

5

Appetite

A sick person often refuses to eat. This is especially frustrating to those who take care of him. Feeding an ill person is the equivalent of nurturing and caring for. We recognize that food—good food—is what gives us strength and stamina to fight off disease and injury. Foods for the seriously ill should be nutritious but light. In some cases, there is a certain bodily wisdom at work in the sick person that aims at stifling the appetite to a certain extent. This should be respected. Force should never be used to make anyone eat when his body tells him not to. But, often, it is the gases that accumulate in the abdomen during a time of lying abed that are the cause for the loss of appetite. When these gases are relieved, the desire for food may well return.

But even those of us who believe we are healthy—or at least not obviously ill—sometimes suffer from a lack of appetite. This is not a sign of health. A few minutes of shiatzu treatment in the morning before rising will help to dissipate this condition and return the appetite to normal. A good appetite does not mean that you will necessarily overeat and gain unwanted pounds. Very often, overweight people suffer from a poor metabolism. The food they eat is not burned up as it should be. Fat then begins to accumulate. Overweight people are also prone to eat the wrong kinds of food, depending heavily upon sugars and carbohydrates. While shiatzu itself cannot bring about a weight loss—this must be accomplished by eating proper foods, preferably proteins, and by getting sufficient exercise—it can help to regulate the metabolism so that the food eaten will be used properly.

One woman we know ate literally nothing until dinner time, yet never lost a pound. She did this for years until she became convinced that she was simply eating the wrong kinds of foods and changed that. But her desire to eat at all, after years of starving herself, was poor until she began to use shiatzu treatments. Now, she eats well, feels better, and maintains her weight with no difficulty.

To increase your appetite, or that of an ill person who refuses all nourishment, take a few minutes daily to administer the following treatment. Stretch out on your back. Press the pit of your stomach for about three seconds with the three fingers of both hands. Repeat this procedure three times (fig. 36). Then move down your abdomen a little and press in the same way three times again. Do this one more time even a little farther down—at about waist level. Now, press on two points to the left of the original point of pressure and on two points to the right. Press each of these points three times (fig. 37). Finally, placing the palm of one hand over the pit of your stomach and the other palm on top of the other hand, press firmly for thirty seconds. Your desire to eat should return after a few days of this treatment.

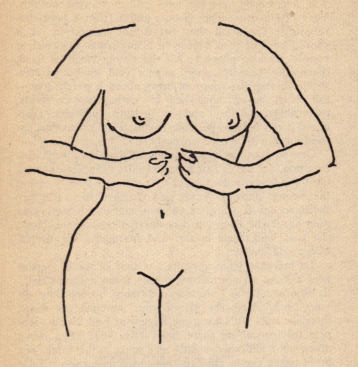

Fig. 36: Pit of stomach

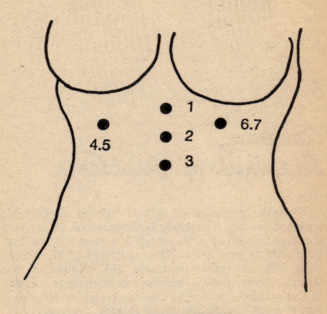

Fig. 37: Gastric region

6

Asthma, Respiratory Problems

While the treatment for asthma requires the help of a second person, we include it because one of our acquaintances with an asthmatic child claims that she has been able to help her child in the relief of his symptoms with this simple treatment. She administers the treatment twice a day—once in the morning and again in the evening—and feels that his breathing has been easier since she began these shiatzu treatments six months ago. On days when an attack seems imminent, she increases the number of treatments. In general, her child's attacks have been less severe.

Two treatments are necessary. In the first, the asthmatic person should lie on his stomach. Press the five points located between the shoulder blades and the spine, being careful to press neither the spine itself nor the shoulder blades. Use both thumbs, one on top of the other, and press each point on both sides three times each (fig. 38). Next, press the three points located on either side of the back of the neck. (See fig. 26.) Press each point lightly for three seconds three times. Now, have the patient lie on his back with a pillow under his head and proceed to give a full treatment of the chest.

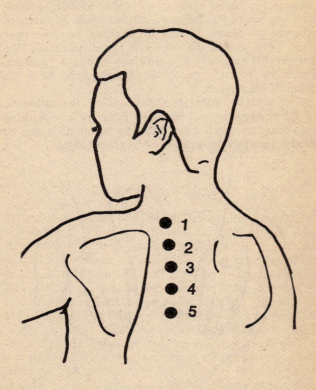

Fig. 38: Points between shoulder blades & spine

Press the five points located on the sternum (fig. 24), beginning at the topmost point and pressing each one three times for three seconds. Using figure 24 as your guide to the location of the points, press all of these lightly, once each, remembering not to press on the ribs themselves. Next, using your palms, gently massage the breast areas in a circular motion as illustrated in figure 39. Repeat each full circle of massage pressure ten times. Finally press down on the upper chest twice so that the patient is forced to exhale. Do not do this suddenly nor with too strong a pressure. Finish by pressing gently on his abdomen with the palms of your hands.

This shiatzu treatment should relieve the asthmatic of the congestion and resultant difficulty in breathing that bring so much discomfort. In addition, it can be used for congestion brought on by chest colds.

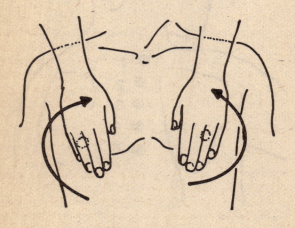

Fig. 39: Massaging the breasts

7

Bed-Wetting

Why is it that some children, at even a very young age, remain dry throughout the night, while others are incontinent? Bed-wetting in toddlers is not so uncommon, and parents are usually patient in dealing with what they believe to be a period of adjustment. But, as a child grows older and continues to have "accidents" at night, the situation becomes one of irritation and concern. Often, the problem is explained as having a psychological basis. This makes it more of a matter for parental worry.

Bed-wetting may indeed be a symptom of inner problems the child may have, and the parents should be careful of their own behavior with the child around his bedtime. It should be a time of calm; it is definitely not a time for chastising or upsetting the child. When difficulties arise between parent and child close to bedtime, it is beneficial if these can be resolved before the child is sent off for his night's rest. He should be reassured that all is well in his world, as difficult as this may sometimes be. Parents should also be firm in the limiting of liquids for several hours before bedtime. Be sure also that the child is dressed warmly, so that he will not get chilled during the night.

Some children are chronic bed wetters all the way into their teens. This is as much an embarrassment to them as it is to their parents. You must be firm but tactful with such a child—and give him a chance. His condition may not stem from psychological problems, but from physical sources. Try the following shiatzu treatment for such a child.

First, press with your thumbs, the five points on the lower back as illustrated in figure 42. Press each point gently but firmly three times. Then press the three points in the region of the buttocks, also illustrated in figure 42. Have the child turn over and, with the palm of your hand, press gently over the lower abdomen and particularly over the area of the bladder. Finish the treatment by pressing on the medulla oblongata (fig. 26) three times to the count of five.

Let your child know that this shiatzu treatment is intended to help him not wet the bed. Children are usually delighted to cooperate with such a positive attitude. And the results are usually quite positive, too. Be sure to administer this treatment at bedtime and for a long period of time, not just for the short while your child might remain dry as a result of several of these treatments. The treatment on the above points helps to stimulate a more normal reaction in the sphincter muscle of the bladder and takes time to be permanently effective.

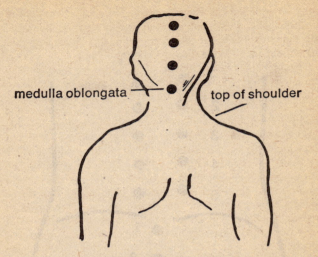

medulla oblongata

top of shoulder

Fig. 40: Points on top of shoulders

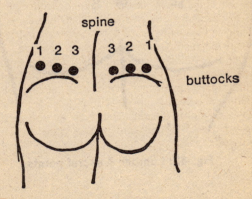

spine

1 2 3   3 2 1

buttocks

Fig. 41: Points above buttocks

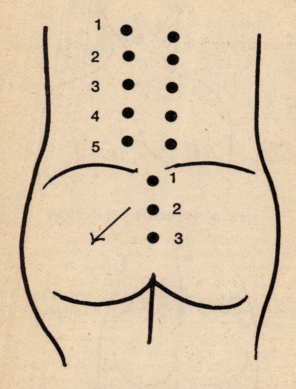

Fig. 42: Lumbar & sacral points

8

Blood Pressure

If you are suffering from high blood pressure, then you had best spend whatever time is necessary for giving yourself the full shiatzu treatment as outlined in chapter 3. Such treatment will help keep all of your muscles flexible and, consequently, your entire circulatory system will benefit. Remember that shiatzu is basically a balancing therapy, one designed to keep fit the normal human biosystem. It is never meant to be used in place of medicine in cases of serious disorders. High blood pressure is a serious disorder. Use shiatzu to work *with* your doctor's recommendation, not in place of it.

In addition to the full treatment, we offer the following supplemental exercises. First, using your three fingers, press the point located in your armpit (fig. 18). Press this point for three seconds three times. Do both sides of the body.

Now, with your thumb, press the point located just beneath your jaw where you can feel your pulse. Press gently and count to ten. Release your pressure, breathe deeply a few times, and repeat this procedure three times on each side of your neck. Next, press the spot over the medulla oblongata, located just at the base of your skull (fig. 26). Use the three fingers of both your hands and press to the count of ten. Repeat this three times. Now press on the three points located on either side of the back of your neck (fig. 26), again using your three fingers. Again, repeat three times. Now press with the three fingers of both hands into the pit of your stomach, to the count of ten. End your treatment by pulling on the middle fingers of both hands, first the left, then the right.

While low blood pressure is never usually as serious as its opposite, it is nevertheless a malfunction of your system and should be treated. Press the point below the jaw the same as in the treatment for high blood pressure. This spot, located over the carotid arteries, is important in regulating blood pressure; therefore, it is a key shiatzu point. Then press the three points on the back of the head as illustrated in figure 26. Press with your three fingers and repeat the procedure three times. Finally, press the points on the shoulder as shown in figure 40.

9

Chills

Any of the following exercises will help to relieve chills. We, ourselves, usually employ several or all of them.

Start with your toes and press the three points on each of your toes, beginning with the base point on the big toe. (See fig. 4.) Next, press all the points on your instep between the bones (fig. 5). Start with the four points located at the base of your toes, pressing each point once. Then press the next four points above this row and so on up toward your ankle. Press to the count of three. Press the four points on the sole of your foot (fig. 6) three times each. Use both thumbs, one on top of the other, and press the third point, the one located in the arch of your foot, with greater pressure. Follow this, by pressing the three points on each side of the ankle (fig. 7). Now, starting at the point just below the knee, press all points on the side of the leg down toward the ankle (fig. 8). Use both thumbs and press each point three times. Again, starting at the topmost point, press the points located on the back of the thighs. Use three fingers for this. (See fig. 9.) Finally, press the three points located just above the buttocks, moving toward the spinal column (fig. 41). For this exercise, you may employ your thumbs. Press each point firmly for three seconds and repeat the procedure three times on each point.

10

Constipation

Hundreds of thousands of Americans suffer from chronic constipation. And many thousands more suffer from an occasional bout with the painful symptoms of this common disorder. Laxatives provide one answer to the problem. But the laxative itself may become part of the problem if you begin to use one regularly. You find that you simply cannot evacuate your bowels without the aid of one of these nonprescription medicines. This is a highly abnormal situation and should be treated immediately!

Part of the problem is, again, the food you eat. Keep a record of all the foods and beverages you consume for a period of two weeks. Then analyze your diet to see how much fiber you are getting. If you are eating the typical American diet of highly processed foods, then you are probably getting very little fiber at all— roughage, as it was once called. You read a lot today about the value of bran and whole grains. Pay attention to that, and begin to change the kinds of foods you are eating, so that you are sure you are getting a sufficient amount of roughage.

Whether you change your diet or not, the following shiatzu exercise will help you. We strongly urge you, however, to become aware of your diet!

In the morning, before rising, press the point illustrated in figure 43, using your three fingers and pressing with both hands for about three minutes. You may find a lump in this area. Rub with your fingers while you press. Do not be surprised to hear some rumblings and gurglings as you do this. It is in this area, called the sigmoid flexure, where the feces tend to collect and stagnate in the large intestine. The pressure you apply sometimes causes a noisy reaction in this area. Drink a glass of water with the juice of half a lemon squeezed into it—fresh lemon, not canned, and no sugar, please! Then wait a half-hour before you eat. If you follow this routine faithfully, your constipation should cease to be a problem for you.

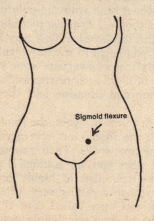

Fig. 43: Point over Sigmoid Flexure

11

Diarrhea

The causes of diarrhea are many. Some are serious, some temporary; but anytime you have diarrhea for more than a day or two, you should check with your doctor for its cause. We have found both yogurt and fasting to be of help. The yogurt should be of the plain variety, and fasting should be of a short duration. And, naturally, we always apply the following shiatzu treatment, which is helpful in relieving diarrhea caused by a malfunctioning of the reflex nervous system. If all these methods fail, and they usually do not, we then see our doctor.

First, press the points located between the spine and shoulder blades on both sides (figure 38). Press for three to five seconds each, three times. Also press the point above the medulla oblongata three times for three seconds (fig. 44). Move down the back and press the five points on either side of the spine as illustrated in figure 42. Continue by pressing the three points located in the buttock area (fig. 42). With both thumbs, one on top of the other, press the point located on the outside of the hip as shown in figure 45. Now press the points on the outer sides of the thighs (fig. 12) and those located on the front of the lower leg (fig. 8). Press all these points for three seconds each and three times each. Now, using both thumbs, apply pressure to the point located between the first two toes of each foot (fig. 46). Do this five times to each foot to the count of five. Finally, use your palm to gently press the lower abdomen for about thirty seconds.

If diarrhea persists after three of these shiatzu treatments, we recommend that you consult your doctor.

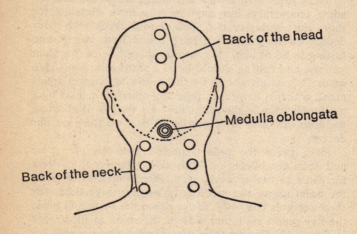

Fig. 44: Back of head & neck

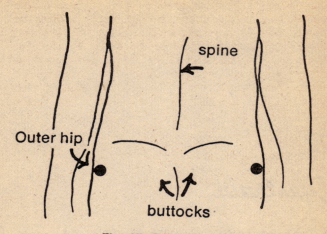

Fig. 45: Outer hip points

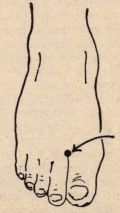

Fig. 46: Point between toes

12

Eyestrain

Too much reading, watching television, close work, or just stress from the daily pressures of your life can affect your eyes to the point where you may not even see as clearly as you normally do. A good night's rest can eliminate these symptoms. Sometimes, however, your eyes feel tired and strained in the middle of your day's activities when it is impossible to just go to sleep. Overworking your eyes will often bring on a headache. To relieve eyestrain and a headache that may accompany it, do the following exercise.

With the three middle fingers, press the upper bony ridge located just under the eyebrow. Use the flat bulbs of your fingers so that your fingernails do not touch the skin. Press three times. Now, using the same fingers, press the bony ridge beneath the eyes, also three times (fig. 30). Once again, press along the upper ridge; but each time you press, move your fingers about a half-inch over in the direction of your ear. Continue pressing along a line that ends just above your ear.

Pressing this line relaxes the muscles around the eye and will result in relief of the strain. Now, massage your temples, moving your fingers in a slow circle. End your treatment by putting the palms of your hands over your eyes. You should not touch the eyeball itself. Your fingers should rest on your forehead, the base of your hand on your cheeks, with your palms forming a cup over your eyes. Close your eyes and relax. You may hold this position as long as you wish—the longer the better.

If you are lying down as you do this last exercise, you may find yourself sinking off into a delightful sleep. If lying prone, rest a pillow on your chest to support your elbows. If sitting, rest your elbows on a table or on some pillows placed in your lap. Also, if sitting, sit erect, using your stomach muscles to support your posture. Slouching only creates strain in other parts of the body and contradicts what you are trying to achieve with the exercises for your eyes.

13

Fevers

Fever is one of the body's signals that something is drastically wrong. So many things may be the cause of the fever that it is difficult for the layman to assess the situation. A fever may accompany the onset of a simple cold, or it may be a symptom of a serious infection or disease. A shiatzu expert, working together with a doctor, can often relieve a fever because he is aware of what is causing it. Unfortunately, the layman is not in this more knowledgeable position. We suggest two exercises that may affect a fever depending on its cause. We ourselves have had both successes and failures with them, but we offer them to our readers for the sake of completeness and in the hopes that they may work for you on at least some occasions.

The first treatment involves the backs of the legs and the Achilles' tendon located at the back of the heel. Starting at the topmost point below your knee, press the eight points on each leg as illustrated in figure 9. Press each point for five seconds and repeat the pro-

cedure three times. Apply pressure to the three points
along the Achilles' tendon in the same way, moving
down toward the heel of the foot (fig. 6). Finally,
press the three points on either side of the ankle (fig.
47), also three times each for the same duration of
time.

If you know, after consulting a doctor, what the
cause of the fever is, you may then apply pressure to
the points that immediately affect those areas.

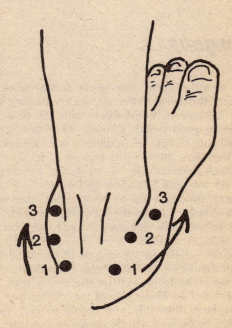

Fig. 47: Points on ankle

14

Hangovers

This small chapter may seem incongruous to the purpose of this book. After all, we are dealing with the delicate balance of our bodies, with the principles of maintaining good health through awareness, diet, and exercise. But let us be practical. And let us not be holier-than-thou. Many, if not most, of us, at one time or another, overindulge in alcoholic beverages. Although we may not intend to do this, we find ourselves at a party, having a sip to be sociable, then another, until the disaster hits us the following morning. If such a thing occasionally happens to you, we recommend the following treatment.

Press the points on the crown of the head as illustrated in figures 48 and 49. Press from the back of the head toward the front, first on the center row, then on the outer rows on either side of this central row. By the time you have done this, you should already be feeling somewhat better and will be happy to continue treating yourself by pressing the points on the front of the neck as illustrated in figure 25. Now, press the three points on your temples (fig. 50), using your three fingers. End your treatment by pressing the three points located on either side of the back of the neck (fig. 25). As usual, press all points for three seconds and repeat each procedure three times.

We sincerely hope that you will not have to use this treatment to cure a hangover very often. Try it sometime when you are simply tired or run-down. It is a real pick-me-up!

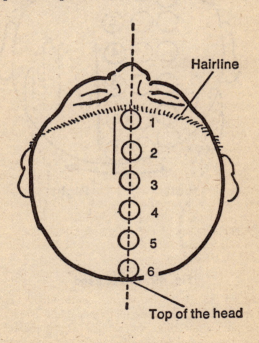

Fig. 48: Top of head

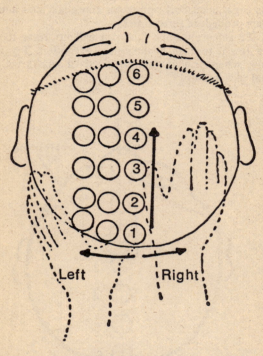

Left   Right

Fig. 49: Top of head

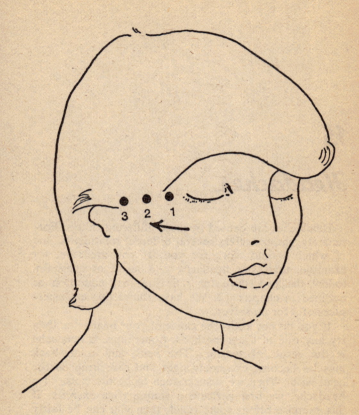

Fig. 50: Temples

15

Headaches

Headaches are caused by many different things. Fortunately, shiatzu offers several different treatments, one of which should work for you. If you are sure, for example, that your headache is a result of eyestrain, follow the procedure for relieving that condition as outlined in chapter 12. We have found this extremely successful for ourselves.

If you do not know the cause of your headache, then try any one of these methods. Sometimes, a headache is the result of tension. The neck and upper-back muscles become extremely tight and can bring on the head pain. When we suspect such to be the cause of a headache, we first perform a simple yoga exercise. If this exercise brings some relief, then you can be fairly certain that the neck area is the source of the difficulty. Here is the yoga exercise. You should do this first, then follow the shiatzu treatment. This usually brings relief.

Sit erect and comfortably. Drop your head forward toward your chest to stretch the back muscles of your neck. Do not pull or strain. Then slowly—this whole exercise should be done very slowly—raise your head and let it fall back as far as you can, again being careful not to strain. Repeat this procedure of moving your head first down toward your chest and then all the way back three times. Now, stretch your neck by dropping your head, first toward the left shoulder, then toward the right and repeat this movement also three times. Now, very slowly, rotate your head in a complete circle in one direction. Repeat three times, then reverse direction and repeat again three times. You will no doubt hear a lot of cracking and feel a pulling in the muscles of the neck. After this preliminary loosening of the neck muscles, you are ready to administer the shiatzu treatment.

First, press the points located on the front of the neck as illustrated in figure 51. Press lightly for three seconds each. Apply pressure three times to each point. Now press the three points located on the back of the neck in the same way (fig. 26). For the front pressure, use your thumbs with your hands around the back of your neck. For the back pressure, use your three fingers with your thumbs pressed against your collarbone. End the treatment by pressing the key points located on the upper shoulders (fig. 40). This helps to loosen the shoulder muscles, which may also be involved in the tension in the neck area. Lie down for at least ten minutes with the palms of your hands covering your eyes as described in chapter 12.

If your headache is caused by neither eyestrain nor tenseness in the neck and shoulder areas, then try these shiatzu treatments. First, press the six points located in the center of the crown of the head. Start with the backmost point and work forward: Press each point three times. Now, press the points located on either side of this median line, first on the left, then on the right. Fgures 48 ad 49 show the locations of these points. Apply pressure to these points four times. You can press them easiest if you use your three fingers. Press again the six points located in the center and repeat three times. Now, using both hands, simultaneously press the points located on the sides six times. End this exercise by once again pressing the center points three times.

Supplement the head-pressure exercise by pressing the points located on the back and front of the neck as described above. In addition to this, press all points located on the instep of the foot as illustrated in figure 5. In this exercise, use your thumbs together, one pressing on top of the other, and work from the base of your toes upward toward the ankle. Press the points across the foot, the four located at the base of the toes first, then moving up to the next row and so on. Press each of these points only once. As with all shiatzu treatments, it is advisable to rest for a short period following the treatment if this is possible.

Fig. 51: Points on the front of the neck

16

Heart Pains, Palpitations, Shortness of Breath

For the purpose of reaching those readers who do not generally read the introduction to a book, we should like to reiterate our warning as stated there. If you suffer from a serious heart condition and the pains you suffer stem from such a condition, do *not* treat yourself with shiatzu! Only an experienced shiatzu expert working together with your own doctor would be able to give you the appropriate treatments. This chapter then is directed toward those people who have been cleared of serious heart disorders by their own doctors yet, for some reason, still suffer from occasional heart pains.

Accompanying such pain there may be shortness of breath, palpitations, or profuse perspiring. Many times the cause of such symptoms is simply stress or anxiety caused by the hectic pace of modern living. Modern psychiatry gives symptoms like these—symptoms without an apparent physical basis—the label of neurotic. We prefer to ignore such labels. The pain is real. The symptoms are physically experienced, and such a label simply adds to the sufferer's feelings of anxiety. Not only does he now have to worry about these symptoms, he must also deal with the belief that he is neurotic as well. So little is known of the human mind and how it and the body truly work together that we feel it is best to forego the simplification of labels! You have physical symptoms. Treat them!

Shiatzu offers several exercises for the treatment of these symptoms. Start first at the top of your head. Press the six points that run down the median line of your crown as illustrated in figure 48. Work from the back to the front of your head. Press each point three times, using the three-finger technique. Next, again using three fingers, press the five points located on each side between the shoulder blades and the spine. If you cannot reach these points yourself, have someone do it for you. Then, reaching around under your armpit, press the point on the shoulder blade itself (fig. 52), paying particular attention to the point on your left side. Press this point three times to the count of five. Now, using the fingers of both hands, press the point over the medulla oblongata (fig. 44). Press to the count of five, three times. Using figures 53 and 54 as your guides, press the points along both upper arms, using the thumb. Again press three times on each point. Now, press the three points located where your chest and the front of your shoulders meet (fig. 55). Use your thumb and apply pressure three times for three seconds. Continue the treatment by pressing the points on the front of the neck (fig. 51). End your treatment by applying pressure to the pit of your stomach (fig. 36) with the palms of your hands. Hold this pressure for ten seconds and repeat three times. Press gently but firmly.

Another exercise that you can do singly anytime during the day is the following. Using figure 22 to find the correct points on your fingers, press each series of points located on the back of each finger with your thumb. Then, using your thumb and middle finger, simultaneously press the points located on the sides of each finger. Press each point once for three seconds and do both hands.

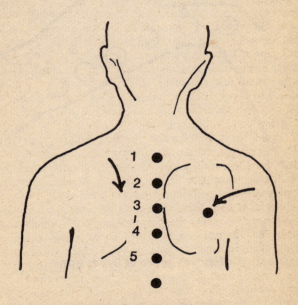

Fig. 52: Shoulder blades

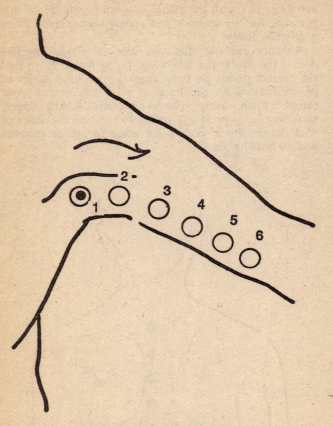

Fig. 53: Inside of upper arm

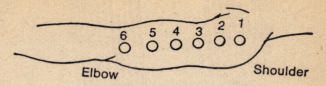

Fig. 54: Outside of upper arm

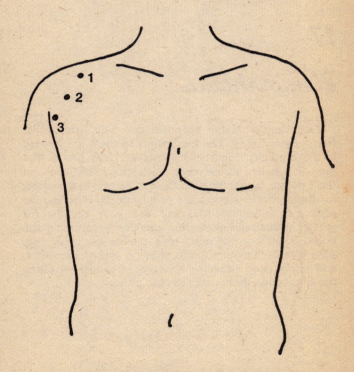

Fig. 55: Area between chest & armpit

17

Hemorrhoids

Two simple shiatzu exercises can help bring relief from hemorrhoids. The first points to press are located in the buttocks. Figure 13 shows the four points that run diagonally across each buttock. Press each of these points, beginning with the first closest to the spine, for five seconds. Repeat the procedure three times. Do each side independently, and use your thumbs for greater pressure. Follow this exercise by pressing the points located on the outer hips, one on each side (fig. 45). Use both your thumbs, one on top of the other, and apply deep pressure for three seconds, repeating the application three times to each point.

18

Hiccups

While hiccups are not usually a symptom of a serious disorder, they can be extremely persistent and irritating. When a case of hiccups occurs, the following shiatzu treatments will usually eliminate them entirely.

Press the three points located on either side of the front of the neck. Using your thumbs, press each point gently three times (fig. 51). Next, press the three points located on the back of the head above the medulla oblongata (fig. 44) also three times each. You will need to use your three fingers to apply pressure to these points. Finally, press the five points—or have someone do this for you—that are located between the spine and shoulder blades (fig. 52). Press the topmost point first, working down from the shoulders. Be careful not to press on either the vertebrae or shoulder blades themselves.

If your hiccups persist, even after these treatments, then a thorough treatment of the abdomen may be required. Press the points as shown in figure 56 first, then those shown in figure 57. Follow the numbers and arrows as you move from point to point. Points with more than one number should be pressed once for each number that appears beside it. Repeat each exercise three times and use your three fingers for these treatments. End the treatment by pressing on the pit of the stomach for thirty seconds, using the palm of one hand.

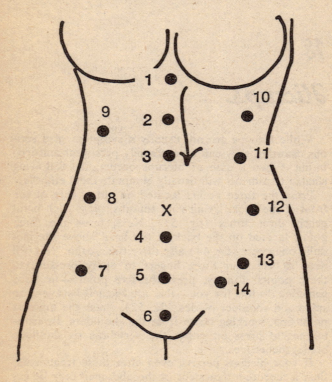

Fig. 56: Abdomen

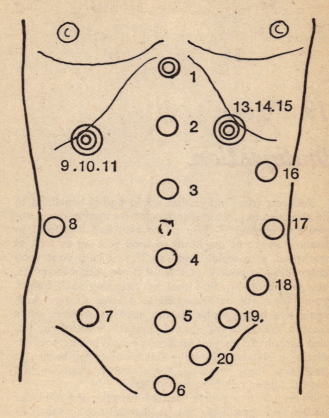

Fig. 57: Points on abdomen

19

Indigestion

Sufferers from indigestion might find it beneficial to do the exercises recommended for improving one's appetite in chapter 5. You might also find it helpful to become aware of the kinds of food you eat as well as the speed with which you eat. If you gulp your food down, chew it poorly, or wash it down with a beverage, you will probably find that by changing such habits, your pains will be alleviated to a large degree. And, again, we must emphasize the need to improve one's diet; in this case, you should eliminate a lot of the fats and carbohydrates you no doubt eat. Whether your indigestion is caused by poor diet, poor eating habits, or neither of these, here are some shiatzu exercises that should help to relieve your problem.

Press the five points located between the shoulder blades and spine (fig. 58). Be careful not to touch either the spine or the shoulder blades and remember to do both sides. Press each point three times for five seconds. Have someone do this first exercise for you if possible. If not, try it yourself, using your three fingers and reaching around over your shoulder. If this is utterly impossible for you, then go on to the next exercise.

First press the point located in the pit of your stomach. Use the three fingers of both hands and press deeply. Then, using figure 56 as your guide to the location of the key points, press each point once for three seconds in the numbered order. Repeat three times. Figure 57 shows the next group of points to be pressed—twenty points in all. Points 9, 10, and 11 as well as 13, 14, and 15 are located in the same place. Press these points three times, all the others only once. Finish this exercise by pressing with the palm of your hand the four points in figure 59. Press each point three times.

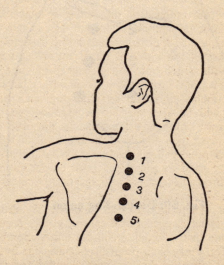

Fig. 58: Points between shoulder blades & spine

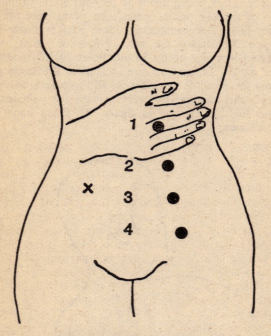

Fig. 59: Descending colon

20

Insomnia

A good night's sleep is probably the best therapy that exists for any condition. Unfortunately, for some people, it is the most difficult therapy to attain. Insomnia creates its own maddening cycle. After one sleepless night, the worry that you will not be able to sleep again produces an anxiety that results in another sleepless night. This can go on and on until the body reaches exhaustion. Sleeping pills do not provide a real answer. In our opinion, they are not only dangerous but also fail in their aim. While you indeed fall asleep after taking one, the sleep you attain is not the same natural therapeutic sleep as that which you achieve on your own.

Whether you suffer from chronic or only occasional insomnia, the following shiatzu exercises will provide great benefit. They help the body and mind to achieve the state of relaxation necessary to a deep and restful sleep.

Lie in bed on your back. First, press the points located on the front of the neck as illustrated in figure 51. Press each point for three seconds and repeat the exercise three times on each side. Use your thumbs to do this. Now, with your three fingers, press the three points located on each side of the back of the neck (fig. 44). Again, do this for three seconds three times. Press the point over the medulla oblongata with your three fingers. Press three times for the duration of five seconds each time. Take a deep breath and stretch your whole body, loosening the tightness you have accumulated throughout the day. End the treatment by pressing once each for three seconds the twenty points located on the abdomen as illustrated in figure 57. Points 9, 10, 11 and 13, 14, and 15 are in the same location. These points should be pressed three times, once for each number.

In addition, you will find it helpful to do the following. Place a pillow on your chest and, resting your elbows there, place your palms over your eyes. Do this in such a way that your palms do not touch the eyeball. They should form a cup over them and should shut out all light. Lie like this for as long as you like. You will soon find yourself completely relaxed and ready for sleep.

21

Knee Pains

Pains in the knees may stem from an old injury, from a sudden jolt or twist, or from no known cause. We find that children between the ages of ten and fifteen frequently complain of such pains. They used to be called growing pains because most children between these ages undergo a great spurt in their growth. Whatever the source, there are several shiatzu treatments that can help relieve the pain. People with recent injuries to their knees should consult first with their doctor as to the advisability of touching the knee. The treatments that do not press directly on the knee itself, however, should be of help in relieving the pain that accompanies a recent injury.

Notice the location of the points on the back of the thigh as illustrated in figure 34. Press the topmost point three times. Apply firm pressure, using your three fingers. Now, move down the back of the thigh, pressing each point three times with slightly less pressure than that applied to the first point. Press once on each of the three points that run behind the knee and repeat this procedure three times. Be sure to start on the outer point and work toward the inside of the leg. Repeat this exercise on the other leg before moving on to the next exercise.

Figure 60 shows the ten points to press on the front of the thigh. Again, beginning at the topmost point, press each point three times, ending at just above the knee. Do the other leg. Now, press the points located around the knee (fig. 61) in the following manner. Start at the bottommost point and press the points going around the left of the kneecap to the topmost point. Press each one three times. Start again at the bottom point and work now on those points going around the right side of the kneecap in the came way. Regulate your pressure according to the pain it may elicit. End the treatment by gently pressing on the kneecap itself with the palm of your hand.

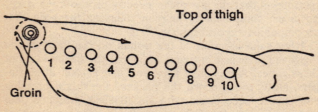

Fig. 60: Top of thigh

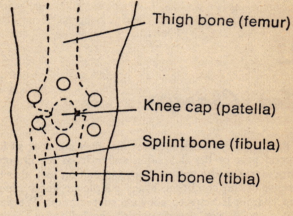

Thigh bone (femur)

Knee cap (patella)

Splint bone (fibula)

Shin bone (tibia)

Fig. 61: Points around knee

22

Leg Cramps

People whose work requires that they stand or sit for a good part of the day often suffer from leg cramps, particularly in the calves. Poor circulation can also be a cause of this condition. Many people we know report that vitamin E helps to alleviate such cramps. We pass that along to you, together with the following shiatzu treatment.

Figure 62 shows you all the points on the backs of the legs that should be your first treatment. Press the topmost point on the back of the thigh three times and press all points below this down to the knee (point ten) once. Repeat this exercise three times. Then, pressing first the point toward the outside of the leg behind the knee, press each of these three points once and repeat three times. End this treatment by pressing all eight points located on the back of the calf also three times each.

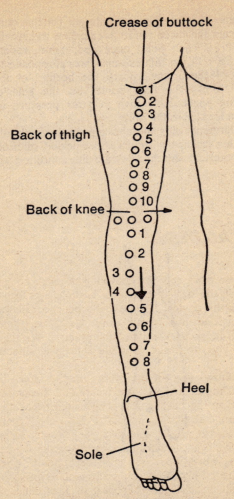

Fig. 62: Points on back of leg

95

The next step in your shiatzu treatment for this condition is to press the three points located on the Achilles' tendon. Press each point once and, again, repeat three times (fig. 63). In this exercise, work opposite to the direction of the arrow toward the bottom of the foot. Finally, press the four points on the sole of the foot, being particularly firm in your pressure on the third point located in the arch.

A daily treatment using the above procedures should relieve your leg cramps within a short period of time. Continued treatment should alleviate the condition entirely.

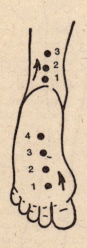

Fig. 63: The sole of the foot and the Achilles' tendon

23

Lumbago

The human back is probably the greatest single source of human misery. Due to our upright posture, we subject our spines and back muscles to a great deal more strain than we do to any other part of our body. We lift, carry, and sag our stomach muscles so that the back holds the full weight of our erect stance. It is not surprising then that there are so many sufferers of one kind of back problem or another. Lumbago is that most common affliction from which we suffer—pain located in the middle and lower back. It can weary one with its constant, nagging pain, or can completely cripple one with sharp, backbending pain that may last for hours, even days.

Shiatzu can help such suffering with daily treatments to the lumbar section of the back and to the area located between the shoulder blades. In addition to the shiatzu treatments, the lumbago sufferer must become aware of his posture and take action to correct it immediately. Even daily shiatzu treatments cannot permanently effect a change if you continue to put all the stress and weight of your body on the back muscles. Pull in your stomach. Exercise to strengthen those muscles, so that your back can get a rest!

Your first treatment should be to the points located alongside the spinal column from mid-back to the lower back. In figure 64, you will see these points, numbered from five to ten. Press point number five first and work downward to point number ten, which should be pressed three times together. Repeat the application of pressure three times. It may also help if you press the three points located on either side of point number ten just above the buttocks. Press the points from the outermost point in toward the spine. Be careful not to press on the vertabrae themselves. The points along the spine are located on either side.

Finish your shiatzu treatment by pressing the five points located between each shoulder blade and the spine. Again, be sure not to press on the skeletal structure. The five points are clearly illustrated in figure 64. Press the topmost point first, then the other four, and repeat the exercise three times. Rest for thirty minutes after the treatment. Lie on your back with a pillow under your knees and one under your head and neck.

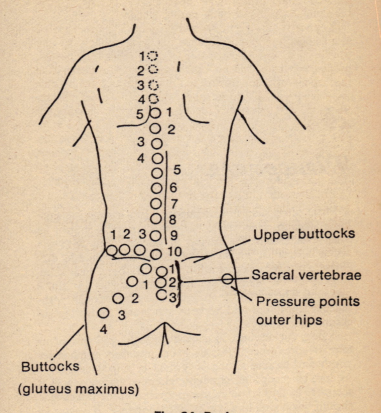

Fig. 64: Back

99

24

Menopause

More often than not menopause is a distressing time for a woman. Her whole body undergoes a change as drastic as that in the period of puberty, but with the opposite results. Physical symptoms may include dizziness, profuse perspiration, hot flashes, headache, ringing in the ears, insomnia, even a rise in blood pressure. These symptoms are distressing enough without the emotional and nervous symptoms that often accompany this period.

Aging, for anyone, is at best difficult, and few of us take it with grace. But, in a culture that emphasizes youth and female allure, it is next to impossible for a woman to accept her changing chemistry with peace! It seems to us that some mental preparation for this period should begin well in advance of menopause. If a woman can approach the menopause with a certain calm, her physical symptoms will be somewhat easier to bear.

The individual woman should carefully examine her own beliefs about approaching old age and compare them with those of the culture in general. Often, her beliefs will coincide with those of the larger world she inhabits. And, in this particular larger world, age is believed to be a time of uselessness, of mental and physical deterioration, and a time when the valued assets of youth are lost forever. But the beliefs of a culture, like those of the individual, are simply beliefs, not facts! The facts of old age, of menopause, of a change in role, are conditioned to a large extent by the individual's whole belief system. If the beliefs can be examined and seen as such, it is possible to change one's future health and mental condition by simply changing the basic beliefs. This must be done at a deep level, however. Simply pretending to oneself that old age is not so bad will not alter one's condition.

The many symptoms of menopause, both physical and emotional, can be greatly altered not only by a deep change in attitude but by a daily shiatzu treatment to particular areas of the body. Key points in these areas affect the glands and organs that bring on the symptoms. By applying pressure to these points, it is possible to relieve the symptoms.

Start with a treatment of the neck and head areas. First, press those points on the top of the head as illustrated in figure 49. Press the points located in the center of the crown of the head first, working from the back to the front. Then, press the points located on either side of this row, first the left side, then the right. Press from the center outward. Press the central row again three times each time. Now press the outer rows simultaneously, using your three fingers to press all of these points on the top of the head.

Figure 44 shows the points to press on the back of the head. With your hands on the top of your head, your thumbs downward, press with one thumb on top of the other. Press the point toward the top of the head first and work down. Repeat three times. Then press the point over the medulla oblongata at the base of the skull, three times for five seconds each time.

Now, press those points on either side of the front of the neck (fig. 51). Be gentle here, but use your thumbs with your fingers behind your neck. Press each point three times for three seconds. Move to the points on the back of the neck (fig. 44) and press each of these points, using the three fingers with your thumbs braced on your collarbone. Again, be gentle and do not exceed three seconds in applying pressure.

With your three fingers, press the points numbered five through ten located in your middle and lower back (fig. 64). Press each point once except for point ten, which should be pressed three times simultaneously. Repeat this exercise three times.

Lie down and proceed with the following treatment of the abdomen. First, press the pit of your stomach (fig. 65) with the palm of one hand, with the other hand on top to add pressure. Press for ten seconds and repeat three times. Now, using figures 56 and 57 as your guides, proceed to press all points, following the numbered order. Those points marked with more than one number should be pressed one time for each number appearing next to it. Each pressure should be three seconds long, and the whole series should be repeated three times. Press the points in figure 56 first; follow with those points in figure 57. These shiatzu treatments, together with a more positive mental attitude, should considerably help any woman to get through menopause with a minimum of difficulty.

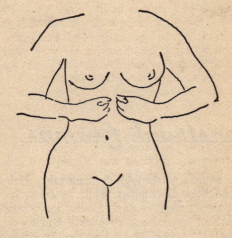

Fig. 65: Pit of stomach

25

Menstrual Cramps

Some women go through their monthly periods without the slightest discomfort, while others suffer agonies of pain, sometimes for days. Breast pain, weakness in the legs, and lower-back pain may add to the misery of abdominal cramps. The causes may be either physical or mental or a combination of the two. Whatever the cause, the pain can be alleviated by using one or more of the following shiatzu treatments. Try different combinations of these exercises to find the ones that work for you.

For the purpose of organization, we will start with exercises of the feet and legs and work up. But you may find a particular organization of your own that works better for you. Try all the exercises the first few times, then experiment with different combinations.

Apply pressure to the points located on the toes (fig. 66). Start with the big toe at the point nearest the foot, and press the three points moving outward toward the top of the toe. End with the little toe. Each application of pressure should be for three seconds, and the exercise should be repeated three times.

Now press the points located on the sole of the foot, as shown in figure 63. Begin pressure on the point closest to the base of the toes and work toward the heel. Apply a stronger pressure on the third point. Repeat this exercise three times. You may use either your thumbs together or your three fingers, whichever is more comfortable for you.

Figure 63 also shows the points to press on the sides of the heel. Press these points in the numbered order, moving in the direction of the arrows. Repeat three times. Continue moving upward and press the six points located on the lower calf alongside the shinbone (fig. 35). Press each point three times for three seconds. Now, press the points located on both the inner and outer sides of the thighs (figs. 67 and 68). Use your thumbs for greater pressure. As usual, repeat each series three times.

Press the three points located over your sacral vertebrae in the lower back between the buttocks. Points pressed in this area will bring almost immediate relief. Use your thumbs to press the points with your hands forward on your hips. Press three times. Proceed to press the four points that cut diagonally across the buttocks and the pressure points located on either side of the outer hips (fig.64). Pressure should be applied with the thumbs to these last two points. Three fingers are most comfortably used to press the points on the buttocks. End treatment in this area by also pressing the three points located just above the buttocks, as illustrated in figure 64 as above.

End your shiatzu treatment by giving yourself a thorough abdominal treatment as outlined in the previous chapter on page seventy-seven. It is best if these treatments are given a few days in advance of the menstrual cycle and continued during the first few days when menstrual pain is usually the strongest.

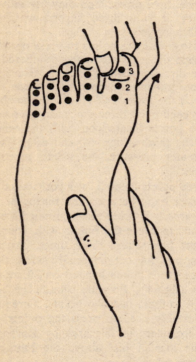

Fig. 66: Points on toes

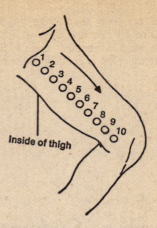

Fig. 67: Inside of thigh

Fig. 68: Outside of thigh

26

Morning Sickness, Nausea

If you are suffering from either of these conditions, you will need the aid of another person to administer the first of these shiatzu treatments. Lie on your stomach. Each of the five points located on either side of the spine between the shoulder blades must be pressed. Have your assistant press each point for five seconds, using his full body weight on both thumbs, one placed on top of the other. If, at any point, you notice a painful spot or if your assistant finds a lump, have him press that point, rubbing slightly to help dissipate the lump. Each point should be pressed five or six times. See figure 64 for the location of these points.

This next treatment you can administer yourself. Lie on your back and, with the palm of your hand, gently but firmly press the pit of your stomach. Place one hand on top of the other for additional pressure. Hold for ten seconds, release, and repeat five times. Usually, you will find relief after one or two applications of pressure. After the fifth repetition, stroke this area gently with the palm of one hand.

27

Motion Sickness

Many people, particularly children, find traveling an ordeal to be endured rather than a pleasure. The movement of a car, bus, train, plane, or boat brings on the nausea and light-headedness that accompany the motion of the vehicle. The cause may be the motion itself, fumes from gasoline, or just the anxiety brought on by the trip. Whatever the cause, there are several key points in your body that can completely relieve the symptoms. A few important suggestions outside of shiatzu treatment may also be helpful.

When traveling by plane, try to keep occupied and yawn or chew gum to help relieve the pressure that builds up in your ears. If on a bus, a train, or in a car, be sure to get up and move around occasionally. A car trip can be a pleasure to the sufferer of motion sickness if stops are made every hour or so for brief exercise. Plenty of fresh air inside the car will also hlep. Exercise is important because long hours of sitting, whatever the vehicle of transportation, slows down the circulation and brings on a condition of weariness and sometimes nausea.

Boat travel can be devastating. It is best in this case to lie down, and stay there. If possible, get some fresh air. Eat lightly, and do not drink a lot of liquids.

Whatever the source of your motion sickness, pressing the point located behind your ear, as illustrated in figure 69, should bring immediate relief. Press firmly on this point several times. Then press on the point over the medulla oblongata (fig. 44) and the three points on either side of the back of the neck. Finally, press the pit of your stomach (fig. 65), using the palm of one hand. Place your other hand over this to attain more pressure. Hold this position for ten seconds, release, and repeat for three applications of pressure.

If your motion sickness seems to be brought on by long periods of sitting, hence poor circulation to the head, press in addition to the above points, the topmost point located on the calf (fig. 35). This point is called the *sanri* point in Japanese. *San* means three and *ri* means a distance of roughly seven miles. In old Japan, most travelers made their journeys by foot and, upon covering a distance of approximately seven miles, they would find themselves weary. They would stop to rest and to burn moxa—an herbal preparation made from the leaves of the wormwood plant—over this particular area. Apparently, this brought relief to the weary traveler, and he could then continue on his way. The *sanri* point is a crucial one then, even to the modern-day traveler who sits for perhaps hundreds of miles in the same position. Press it and get relief!

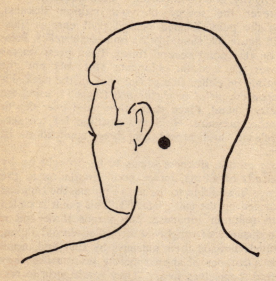

Fig. 69: Point over mastoid process

28

Nasal Congestion, Common Cold

A full treatment of shiatzu everyday is no doubt one of the best preventions you could find against the common cold. That, together with good dietary habits and sufficient exercise, is the best and most formidable defense against the intrusion of germs and viruses into your body. We ourselves simply do not get colds like we used to; and the rare times one seems to be beginning, a few extra precautionary shiatzu treatments relieve the symptoms so that they are short-lived and mild in their effects.

The next time you feel a cold coming on, try treating the face and neck areas. Press the points along the sides of your nose to relieve nasal congestion (fig. 70). Also press the points around your eyes (fig. 30) and across your temples (fig. 31). Always press in the direction of the arrows and numbers. Press each point three times for three seconds. Press the points along your cheek-bones. Now press the three points located on the back of the head as shown in figure 44. Finally, press the points on both the front and back of the neck, being firm but gentle on these points (fig. 44 and 51). These treatments should keep the symptoms under control.

If your cold is already in full sway, then a more complete treatment is necessary. Press the points above and continue with treatment of the calves, thighs, and abdominal areas. Points to press in these areas are illustrated in figures 8, 9, and 57. Press each point three times, using either the thumb or three-finger technique, whichever is more comfortable. Use your palms to press the area over the pit of the stomach. Each point should be pressed for three to five seconds.

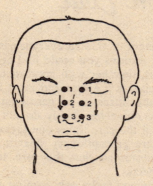

Fig. 70: Nose

114

29

Neck Cramps

Stiffness and pain in the neck area can fairly well incapacitate a person. Treatment on any area of pain, but particularly in the neck, should be extremely gentle. First, hold the palm of your hand over the painful area for a period of time. The warmth from your hand will help to slightly relax the muscles. You may also use a heating pad or warmed cloth to accomplish this.

When the area is somewhat relaxed, very gently press the points closest to it. Generally, the pain will be either in the back or on the sides. Press the back points first (fig. 71), then the sides. Use your three fingers and press each point three times for only three seconds. Never press so that your pain is increased. Continue treatment by pressing the points on the front of the neck as well and end by treating the points located on the top of each shoulder and between the shoulder blades (fig. 52).

When the area feels somewhat relieved, repeat the treatment, pressing a little deeper this second time. You need to get to the deeper muscles. For this, more pressure is necessary. But do not force yourself. If there is great pain, treat with gentle pressure until the pain subsides.

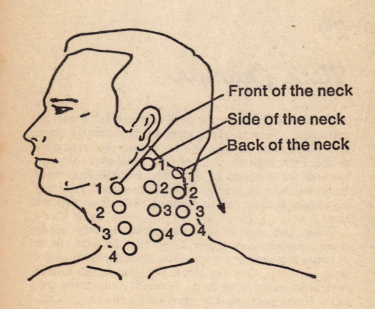

Fig. 71: Neck

116

30

Nervousness

Nervousness may be either physically or mentally caused. It is important for the person to discover, as best he can, the source of his difficulty. Examine yourself. If you have always been a nervous person, it may be difficult for you to alter your state even with shiatzu. Metabolic disturbances, glandular malfunctions, poor diet, stress—a whole panoply of both internal and external factors—may be involved. Check into your diet and physical condition with your doctor. Try to eliminate the stress factors in your life that may contribute to your nervous state. And be sure that you truly want to change. Sometimes, people find it difficult to relax because they are actually more comfortable being tense and high-strung. Examine your value system. Do you feel you are most effective when apparently busy with something? Do you believe that relaxed people accomplish little or are lazy? These kinds of questions are important to your examination of the reasons for your condition.

There are two important areas of shiatzu treatment that can help alleviate nervousness if its cause is physical or of a temporary nature. First, press the points around the eyes and temples (figs. 72 and 73). Do this lying down. Breathe deeply both before and after this treatment. Concentrate your attention on the treatment, not allowing other factors to interfere. Finish this treatment by placing the palms of your hands over your eyes, cuplike, so the palms are not touching the eyeballs themselves. Place a pillow on your chest to support your elbows and hold this position for at least ten minutes.

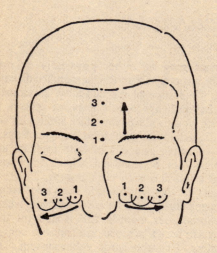

Fig. 72: Eyes
118

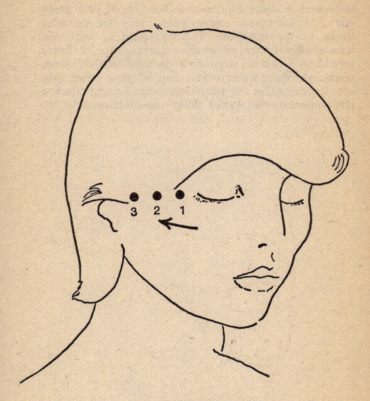

Fig. 73: Temples

Taking a sitting position, with your hands over your shoulders, press the five points located between your spine and shoulder blades on either side of your body (fig. 52). Be careful not to press either the shoulder blades or the vertebrae. This treatment is best done with the assistance of another person. But, if fairly supple, you can do it yourself on most of the points, using your three fingers. At a time of great stress, you may repeat either of these treatments several times a day without any danger of doing yourself harm.

31

Neuralgia

Neuralgia occurs in various parts of the body. There are a number of effective shiatzu treatments for neuralgia. The best rule to follow is to treat those points closest to the source of pain first, then to treat those points farther away. It is often a surprise to find that a distant point may affect the condition more favorably than one closer. The following is an outline of all the treatments you might use.

Press the points located on all parts of the face and head. Start with the points located on the top of the head first as illustrated in figure 49. Move down to the three points on the back of the head (fig. 44). All of the points in these treatments should be pressed three times for three to five seconds unless otherwise indicated. Use your thumb whenever feasible. Otherwise, use the three-finger technique. Always follow the direction of the arrows and the numbered order.

After you have given yourself a thorough treatment of the points on the head and face (figs. 29, 72, 73, and 70), press, for three seconds only, the points located on either side of the back of the neck. Now, press the point on the top of the shoulder, both sides, and the five points located between the shoulder blades and the spine (fig. 52). It is easiest if someone else presses these last points as well as the next. If you have no one to assist you, try reaching them yourself, being careful not to strain. Figure 64 shows the points to press in your middle to lower back. Press points five through ten and be careful not to press on the spine itself. Now press the points located on the outer hip on either side (fig. 45).

The next area to treat is the arms. First, press the point located in the armpits, then all the points in the upper arm (figs. 53 and 54). Finish your treatment with a thorough treatment of the chest and abdomen (figs. 24 and 57).

You may find that your particular neuralgia is benefited by one or two of these treatments. In this case, you may wish to limit yourself to just these. Try experimenting with different combinations. You will surely find the right combination for yourself.

32

Nosebleed

If you suffer from frequent nosebleeds, then we strongly urge you to see your doctor for treatment. For an occasional nosebleed, we recommend the following simple shiatzu treatment.

First, use an ice pack on the nose to slow the bleeding. Use packing in the nostrils if necessary. Then, leaning your head slightly back, press the point over the medulla oblongata (fig. 44). Maintain pressure each time for ten seconds. Release and apply pressure in this way until the bleeding stops.

33

Numbness

Numbness in the arms or fingers can be relieved by a series of shiatzu treatments. First, press the points located on the top of the shoulders (fig. 40). Using either the thumb or three fingers of the opposite hand, press this point three times for three seconds each time. Now, move down to the point located in each armpit and press this point, on each side, in the same way (fig. 55). Use your thumb for this application of pressure. Continue pressing the other points that run down the inner side of the upper arm (fig. 53). Change to the three-finger technique and press the six points located on the outer side of the upper arm as in figure 54.

Continue your treatment by pressing the eight points on the outer forearm (fig. 21). Press the first point three times, all the others only once. But repeat the exercise three times as with all other exercises. Use your thumb on the points of the forearm for greater pressure. Turn your palm up and press the points on the inner forearm (fig. 20) in the following way. Press only once on each point, using your thumb. Press first the nine points that run down the inside in a line above your little finger. Then press the middle row of points and lastly the row above the thumb side of the arm. Do both arms in this way. Finally, press all the points on the thumbs and fingers (fig. 22). Press the middle row of points first. Use your thumb and move in the direction of the numbers and arrows. After pressing the center row on each finger, use your index finger and thumb to simultaneously press the points located on either side of each finger.

If you experience numbness in your legs or feet, the following exercises will benefit you. Using figure 62 as a guide to the points on the back of the leg, press first the ten points located on the back of the thigh. Use the three fingers of one hand. Press the topmost point three times and each of the remaining points once, all for three seconds. Repeat this exercise three times.

Now press the three points behind the knee. Use your thumbs together, one on top of the other, and press the outermost point first, moving toward the inside of the leg. Press each point once, and be firm with your pressure. Move down the back of the calf and press each of the eight points once. Repeat this exercise three times, pressing each point for three seconds. Rest a moment. Then press the three points on the Achilles' tendon (fig. 63). Follow the numbers and arrows. Continue the treatment for numbness of the legs and feet by pressing the three points on either side of the ankle (fig. 47). For both the treatment of the heel and the ankle, apply pressure for three seconds and repeat the exercise three times. Press now the four points located on the soles of the feet, using three fingers for this. Apply stronger pressure on the third point and, again, repeat this exercise three times.

Now, using your thumbs, one on top of the other, press all the points located on the top of your foot (fig. 74). Press all of the points in row one, moving across the foot at the base of the toes, then row two and so on up toward the ankle. In this exercise, press each point only once. Be careful not to press on the bones of the foot itself. The points are located between the bones. End your treatment by pressing, also only once, on each of the points on the toes. Press those on the big toe first, moving toward the little toe (fig. 66).

If the numbness you experience does not flow from a serious disorder, these exercises will greatly aid you in alleviating the condition. By stimulating blood circulation, they reach down to the root of the problem, eliminating it entirely.

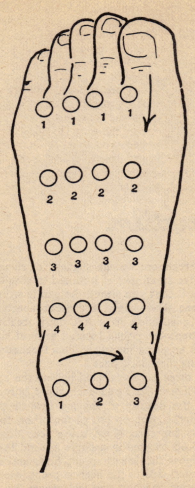

Fig. 74: Points on instep

34

Rheumatism

The best treatment we can suggest for rheumatism is the full shiatzu treatment as outlined in chapter 3. Our only caution is that you should be gentle with pressure in those areas where pain is present—particularly in the joints. In addition to a full daily treatment, you might also treat the points located around and behind the knees as an extra measure. This treatment is helpful in relieving rheumatic pain.

Press the three points located behind the knee, as illustrated in figure 62. Press each point only once and move from the outside of the leg toward the inside. Use both thumbs, one on top of the other, to give you the necessary pressure. Now, using your three fingers, press the points located in a circle around the kneecap (fig. 61). Press the lowest point first, and move upward on the left side to the highest point just above the kneecap. Return to point one and repeat the same procedure on the right side of the knee. Repeat this exercise three times, and end treatment by gently pressing on the kneecap with the palm of your hand. Hold this pressure for ten seconds and release. Be sure to treat both knees.

35

Sciatica

The distress caused by sciatica can be greatly relieved by two shiatzu treatments, one on the thighs, the other on the abdomen.

See figure 67 for the location of the points to press on the inner thigh. Each of these points should be pressed three times for three seconds. You may use either your thumb or three fingers, whichever is more comfortable. Repeat the exercise three times.

The next exercise, on the abdomen, may seem to be a strange one for the treatment of sciatica, but it is greatly helpful in obtaining relief. First, press the eight points as illustrated in figure 75. Follow the numbers and arrows as you apply pressure to these points. Press each one once, and repeat the treatment three times. Use your three fingers for pressing all points on the abdomen. Next, press the twenty points shown in figure 57. Again, follow the numbered order. Where there are three numbers at a point, press three times. Otherwise press each point only once, but repeat the exercise three times.

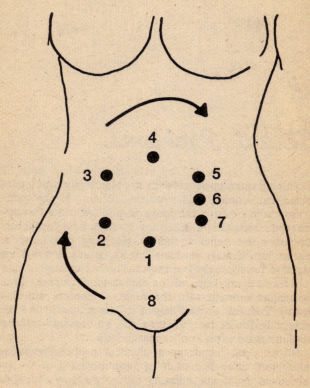

Fig. 75: Points on abdomen

36

Sexual Problems

This chapter is devoted to problems in sexual performance. Women with problems relating to the menstrual cycle or to menopause should refer to the appropriate chapters. Difficulties in sexual performance, for either the male or the female, may stem from a myriad of physical problems or from any number of negative psychological attitudes. Shiatzu treatment can help both, even those with psychological origins. Poor sexual performance—in the male, premature ejaculation or inability to maintain a full erection; in the female, frigidity or inability to reach an orgasm—can be a complicated affair (no pun intended).

Often, what began as a physical problem can escalate into a combination of both physical and psychological problems, creating an unfortunate situation. An inability to perform well in our other functions—digestion, for example—is, of course, a source of distress, but it never arouses guilt or shame in one as does an inability to perform well in the sexual act.

Naturally, the reader is no doubt aware of some of the steps he should take to discover the root of his problem. A physical examination and thorough discussion of the problem with a physician is strongly advised, as well as a good talking-out of the problem with one's partner. The unfortunate part of sexual difficulty is that it brings on problems for one's partner as well as for oneself.

For example, if the man has difficulty maintaining a full erection, hence unable to satisfy the woman, she may, in turn, begin to avoid the sexual act, becoming apparently frigid. And the opposite can have the same sort of effect on the male. The problem escalates then to create a sometimes unbearable situation. Hence, it is most important, if a relationship is to succeed, to solve the sexual problem.

How does shiatzu enter into the solution of such complicated problems as these? We will try to answer that question as simply as possibly. First, as we have stated elsewhere, little is known of the deep relationship that exists between the mind and the body. In Western culture, the tendency has always been to separate the two, almost as if they acted independently of each other. We believe this is not the case. A healthy body, full of vigor and stamina, usually coincides with an equally healthy and energetic mind. Shiatzu works to help the body find and maintain its natural equilibrium. By doing so, it also lends to a more balanced functioning of the mind. The two parts are not really separate—they are one! Thus, by treating your body with shiatzu, you are also treating your mind. In this apparently indirect way then, shiatzu affects your mental attitudes and condition. To our great surprise, mental problems often disappear as the body is brought back into balance.

Now, there are points within the body that affect the

balance of hormones and the functioning of the sexual organs. These are the key points in your treatment. But we would also urge you to make use of the full shiatzu treatment as outlined in chapter 3. Sometimes a malfunctioning in the sexual organs or negative attitudes of the mind are brought on by malfunctions in other parts of the body and the accompanying disorders, imbalances, and fatigue that these generate. Such imbalances will also affect your sexual staminia and potency.

As you work with full shiatzu treatments, be sure to give yourself these following sex-related shiatzu treatments. Except for the treatment of the toes, which is specifically aimed at frigidity in women, all the treatments can be employed by both men and women. These exercises help both sexes to perform better, and will relieve frigidity, hormone imbalances, and sexual weakness such as maintaining a full erection or premature ejaculation.

The first areas to treat are in the area of the back and buttocks. Press points five through ten located in the lumbar region of the back as illustrated in figure 64. Each point should be pressed once, except for point ten, which you must press three times. Repeat the exercise three times also. Use your thumbs, your hands wrapped around your rib cage and waist, or have someone help you with these points on the back. Next, press the three points that run down the tailbone. Use three fingers for this treatment if you have no one to assist you, and press each point three times. Continue treatment in this area by pressing, again three times each, the four points that run diagonally across the buttocks on either side. Also press the three points horizontal to point ten on the lower back. End the treatment of the back area by pressing the points located on either side of the outer hips (fig. 45). Press this point once, using deep pressure.

Lie down or sit, and press all the points on the abdomen as illustrated in figures 56 and 57. Follow the numbered order and the arrows in the movement of your pressure. Press the points in figure 56 first, and follow with treatment of the points in figure 57. Where there is more than one number at a point, press the point that number of times. For this treatment you will have to use the three-finger technique. End this treatment by placing the palm of one hand over the pit of the stomach and, with the other hand on top for added pressure, press for thirty seconds.

The next treatment involves the inner thighs. Use figure 67 as your guide to the key points. Press each of the ten points once, using the thumb. Repeat three times. Now, with the palm of your hand, press the point located over the groin (fig. 10). Pressure in this area should be applied gradually, and should be gentle. Repeat this pressure three times.

In case of frigidity, it is also helpful, in addition to the above treatments, to apply pressure to the toes. Begin with the big toe, the inside point, and press each of the three points once. Go on to the next toe and so on to the little toe. Repeat this treatment three times. (See fig. 66.)

37

Sinusitis

For quick relief of sinusitis, press the points located along both sides of the nose (figure 70). Use your thumbs and press the points according to the numbers and arrows. Next, press the three points located in the center of the forehead. In this case, you will be working in the opposite direction from the treatment you administered on the nose points. Press the point closest to the eyes first, and move toward the top of your head (fig. 29). In both cases, press each point three times for three seconds.

Now, continue treatment by pressing the points located in a center line across the top of the head (fig. 48). Press each of these points three times also. Work from the forehead toward the back of the head. You will have to use the three-finger technique to accomplish this. Press also, three times, the three points on the back of the head, then the point over the medulla oblongata (fig. 76). Still using your three fingers, press once the point located on the top of each shoulder as shown in figure 40. End your treatment by gently pressing each of the points located on the front, back, and sides of the neck. These points are illustrated in figures 71 and 76. These treatments may be done three or four times a day to relieve discomfort and congestion.

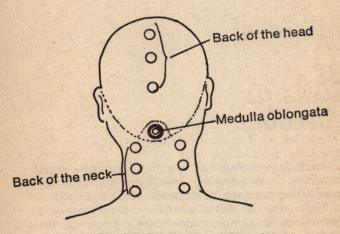

Fig. 76: Back of head & neck

38

Swelling

Swelling in the legs and feet that occurs as a regular condition or as a result of insufficient exercise can be greatly helped by shiatzu treatment of the legs and feet.

First treat the points located on the backs of the lower legs. These points are shown in figure 62. Press each point three times, starting at the one just below the knee and moving down the leg toward the foot. After this treatment, continue pressing the three points located on the Achilles' tendon (fig. 63), moving in the same direction. Now, press the four points located on the sole of each foot (also fig. 63). Press the point nearest the toes first, and move back toward the heel. Each point should be pressed three times, and greater pressure should be exerted on the third point located in the arch. Be sure to do both legs and both soles. Done three times a day, these treatments are very helpful in controlling swelling.

39

Toothache

Pain is always a signal to us that something is amiss somewhere. A toothache should alert you to immediately get in touch with your dentist and have the tooth examined and treated. Shiatzu cannot cure a bad tooth. But it can greatly reduce the pain that derives from a bad tooth. We strongly recommend the following treatments but, also as strongly, we recommend that you see your dentist even if the pain is entirely eliminated.

First, press the part of the cheek that is located immediately above the sore tooth. Use your forefinger with your middle finger pressing on it to gain greater pressure. Hold this position until the pain begins to lessen. Next, press with your thumb along the lower jaw as far as the ear on the side of the face where the pain is (fig. 77). On the same side, press the point on the side of the neck just below the jaw. Finally, press the points located on the temple (fig. 73), also on the side of the toothache. Press each of these three times, using your three fingers. If your pain persists, repeat the first procedure until it diminishes.

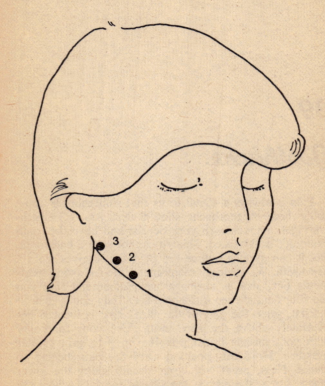

Fig. 77: Jaw

40

Whiplash

Whenever you suspect that you have received even a slight whiplash, you should give yourself the shiatzu treatment as outlined in this section. Naturally, if the whiplash is severe, you should immediately see your doctor as well. Sometimes it takes a few days before the effects of a whiplash injury appear. By treating yourself immediately, you may circumvent later pain.

Press the points located on either side of the front of the neck as shown in figure 78. Use your thumbs and press each point gently three times. Next, press the points on the sides of the neck (fig. 71). Using your three fingers, press the points located on the back of the head and over the medulla oblongata (fig. 76). Press three seconds on each and repeat the exercise three times. Continue by pressing the points on the back of the neck in the same way. Finally, press the point located on each upper shoulder (fig. 40), also using your three fingers. Press this point once to the count of five. When pain is present, use caution and apply pressure gently and gradually. As pain subsides, you may use greater pressure on subsequent treatments.

Fig. 78: Points on the front of the neck

41

Writer's Cramp

As we draw to a close in our writing of this book, it seems appropriate to end with a treatment for writer's cramp. It is a treatment we can happily recommend, one we have used frequently with great success! While called writer's cramp, it could just as well be called clerk's or secretary's cramp. Anyone doing a lot of paper work is familiar with the fatigue of the forearms one suffers from such work.

Treat the points along the forearm as shown in figure 79. Press the nine points that run down the inside of the forearm first. Use your thumb and press each point once only. Press the nine points in the middle row, then those in the outside row. Next, treat the points located in the thumbs and fingers (fig. 22). With your thumb, press first the central row of points on the other thumb. Then, using your forefinger and thumb, simultaneously press the points on both sides. Continue this procedure with the other fingers. If just

143

one arm is painful, as is usually the case, you need only treat that one side. But be sure to press all of these points three times each. After such a treatment, your pain and fatigue will be greatly relieved.

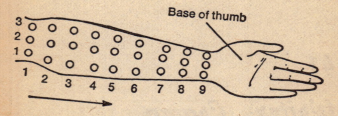

Fig. 79: Inside of forearm